CHILDREN OF THE WOLF

Look for all the books in

THE WEREWOLF CHRONICLES

trilogy:

Book I: *Night Creature*

Book II: *Children of the Wolf*

Book III: *The Wereing*

THE WEREWOLF CHRONICLES

CHILDREN OF THE WOLF

Book II

Rodman Philbrick and Lynn Harnett

AN
APPLE
PAPERBACK

SCHOLASTIC INC.
New York Toronto London Auckland Sydney

ISBN 0-590-69240-2

12 11 10 9 8 7 6 5 4 3 2 1   6 7 8 9/9 0 1/0

Printed in the U.S.A.   40

First Scholastic printing, August 1996

For Fin Hansen

RULES OF THE WEREING

1. A werewolf is created by birth or bite.

2. The wereing is the change from human to beast and lasts for the three nights of the full moon.

3. The first wereing of a werewolf child occurs in the twelfth year.

4. If the werewolf child makes a kill in the three nights of the full moon, it shall have all the powers of a full-blooded werewolf and remain a monster forever.

5. A full-blooded werewolf can change into human form at any time, but must become a werewolf when the moon is full.

6. A werewolf cannot cross water.

7. A werewolf cannot tolerate anything silver.

Chapter 1

I am a monster. The humans don't know my secret, or they would never have saved me. They found me in the swamp as they hunted the wolves — my real family — and brought me to this strange place they call a *town*.

They say they want to raise me as a human. They say they want to save me. But these poor, weak humans don't know the danger they've allowed into this wooden den they call a *home*.

The danger is me.

I can't help it. On the first evening of the full moon the Change comes over me and I turn into a foul creature of the night. A werewolf. A monster so terrifying that even my brave Wolf-mother fled in fear. A monster so ghastly, so powerful, that it can see in the dark, and hear the heartbeat of a frightened bird on the wing. A monster whose glistening fangs ache for blood.

The most terrifying thing of all is that I am not alone. The night is full of monsters like me. By day they look human, act human. But at night they raise their human faces to the moon and turn into werewolves. And then in the darkness they hunt their victims, preferably children. . . .

"Gruff! Are you okay in there?"

That was Paul, the boy whose parents had taken me into their home. He was outside this part of the den they call a *bedroom*, knocking on the wooden shield the humans call a *door*.

"Ohh-kayyy," I managed to growl. It wasn't easy getting the human words to work inside my throat, but I was trying. I wanted to please these humans. I especially liked Paul and his sister Kim.

"Take your time," Paul called out. "You'll get used to it."

He meant that I would get used to living with humans. I wasn't so sure. Maybe they'd never get used to me! After all, I'd never lived with humans before. Even though I was a human boy I had been raised by wolves since I was small, and lived and hunted as a wolf. I didn't know the ways of humans — and they didn't know me.

It had been a very long day. I was so tired it felt like the walls of this strange room were pressing in on me. So I went to the window to look out on my old home — the swamp.

As I looked out into the night from the second-floor window something caught my eye. A man. He was moving from shadow to shadow as if he was trying not to be seen.

Something about the way he moved made the hair stand up on the back of my neck. I had to force myself not to growl or bark. I was with the humans now — all I could do was stand watch over them.

So I watched intently as the man moved from the shadows and headed for the woods. Before he got there he stopped in a silvery patch of moonlight. Like he was waiting for someone.

A minute or so later the shadows moved again, and four more men scurried out of the darkness and joined him. They all stood there in the moonlight, waiting.

I shivered as if a worm had crawled up my spine, but I couldn't stop staring at them. I wanted to turn away from the window but I felt something was about to happen. Something I needed to know.

Suddenly my breath caught in my throat.

The men's faces were changing! As I watched, their ears grew long and pointed. Their mouths and noses fused into long snouts. Suddenly they threw back their heads and howled.

Werewolves!

Chapter 2

I watched, frozen with horror, as their clothes burst at the seams and fell away from their bodies. They dropped to all fours, sprouting wiry gray fur. They twisted and writhed in the moonlight as muscles rippled under flesh.

When the Change was complete the werewolves crouched motionless for a moment, as if savoring the change.

Then, all together they swung around and looked at me.

Five pairs of glowing red eyes glared up at my window. The monsters grinned at me, showing sharp yellow fangs.

I ducked back out of sight but it was too late. The werewolves had seen me!

Pressed against the wall, I heard a low, vicious laugh from outside.

"Join us, little Gruff," they called in a chorus of voices that dripped with evil. *"Join us, or die!"*

I whimpered in fear as the horrible voices echoed inside my head. I couldn't move. It was like I was paralyzed.

I looked down at my own body but it stayed normal. Frozen with terror and dread I waited for the tingling in my arms and legs that meant I was changing into a werewolf, too, just like I had for the past three nights.

But nothing happened. I slumped in relief. The moon was no longer full. I would remain a boy until the next full moon. But it horrified me to realize that full werewolves — those who had made a kill — could change at any time!

When my own hammering heart stopped pounding in my ears I heard the creatures whispering among themselves. Then suddenly everything went quiet. Had they gone? I was afraid to look.

But I had to know. Very slowly I inched my head toward the window and peered out.

Four hairy monsters were huddled in a corner of the yard.

Four? A minute ago there had been five of them out there. Where was the fifth werewolf? What was it doing?

I jerked my head back, afraid to breathe. But maybe I had counted wrong. It was dark out there, maybe I missed one. Biting my lip, I cautiously peeked out again.

No. I had counted right. There were four werewolves crouched in the yard, facing the house as if they were waiting. Their fangs gleamed in the moonlight and dripped with anticipation.

The monsters were plotting something and I was the only one who knew they were here. I was the only one who knew they even existed.

They were humans by day and evil monsters by night.

I had seen them as monsters before, for three nights in the woodsy swamp behind the town. They wanted me to kill, to become a full-blooded werewolf, and I almost had.

But last night the werewolves had come out of the swamp and stolen a child from the town. I had followed them and stopped them from hurting the child and chased them back into the swamp.

I thought the creatures came from the swamp. Now I knew they lived right here in town.

But the other townspeople didn't believe in monsters. They blamed the real wolves who lived in the swamp — the beautiful gray wolves who were the only family I could remember. The wolves had taken me in when I was a baby and I could never let anyone hurt them.

At dawn the humans from town had sent out men with guns to hunt my wolf family down. The hunters hadn't killed my family but they did capture me — the "wolf-boy" who lived with the wolves.

And now they were trying to make a human boy out of me.

And I knew I'd much rather be a human than a monster. In my heart I was a human, I was!

Now the werewolves had come for me.

SCRREEEEEEK.

It was the sound of a claw scraping against the outside of the house below my window.

The werewolf was climbing up the side of the house!

THUMP! SCRRAATCH!

It slipped and grunted as its claws scrabbled for a hold. I waited for the sound of its body hitting the ground. Nothing.

Then I heard the faint scratching, clicking sound again. It hadn't fallen.

And it had climbed much closer. I could hear the rasp of its breath.

It was coming to get me!

Chapter 3

I screamed and bolted for the bedroom door.

"Paul!" I shouted into the hallway. "H-help! Help!"

Paul's bedroom door flew open. "What?" he cried. "What's the matter?"

Paul was my age, twelve. His brown eyes were wide-open as he hurried toward me. But he didn't look scared, just concerned. Paul's family had taken me in that morning when the hunters brought me out of the swamp.

I opened my mouth but no words came out. Paul looked over my shoulder, into the dark bedroom. I put my hand on his arm to stop him from going in to look.

"No," I said haltingly, in my rusty voice. "Wait for the dad."

We could both hear Mr. Parker's feet pounding up the stairs. Mrs. Parker was right behind him and Kim, Paul's younger sister, was behind her.

"What's wrong, boy?" Mr. Parker asked me. Mrs. Parker looked worried.

"He thinks there's something scary in his room!" said Paul, the words tumbling out of him in excitement.

Mr. Parker frowned. He was a big man with a serious expression. "Let Gruff speak for himself, Paul," he said.

"But, Dad, you know he can't," said Paul, hopping from foot to foot impatiently. He was eager to get into my room and see what scared me. "He's been brought up by a family of wolves his whole life. We can't expect him to learn English in one day."

"Well, he won't learn if you don't let him try." Mr. Parker turned to me. "Now, Gruff, can you tell me what happened?"

I pointed at the bedroom. Even though I could understand a lot of the human talk, it was much harder to sort all my jumbled thoughts into words and get my lips and tongue to make the right sounds.

"Werewolves," I said. "Inside. You see."

I grasped Mr. Parker's hand and pulled him into the room. I pointed at the window. "There!"

Mr. Parker exchanged a glance with his wife. She shrugged her shoulders and nodded. I could tell neither of them believed me.

Mr. Parker walked over to the window in two long strides. Feeling safer with him there, I followed.

"Sorry, Gruff, but I don't see a thing," said

9

Mr. Parker as he peered into the night. "Seems pretty quiet out there."

The werewolves had disappeared.

"Perhaps you had a nightmare," said Mrs. Parker in her soft friendly voice. "It's your first night in a strange place. You've never been in a house before, have you, Gruff?"

I shook my head, "No." I had, once long ago before I was left with the wolves, but it was too complicated to explain and I didn't really remember what it was like.

"Well then," she said, satisfied. "It's only natural you'll have scary dreams the first few days."

There wasn't any way I could convince them. But at least the werewolves were gone.

Then I saw a stealthy movement out of the corner of my eye. A big shadow, lurking behind the bushes near the street.

I grabbed Mr. Parker's sleeve and pointed. He peered intently into the darkness. Then his face relaxed and he smiled. "That's Mr. Ford, our next-door neighbor," he said, ruffling my hair. "He's out walking his dog, Misty. And Misty is hardly a monster."

Misty the dog was very small and fluffy and waddled when it walked. Mr. Ford was about a hundred years old. I felt embarrassed. Now I'd ruined any chance I had of ever convincing them that the werewolves were real!

Mr. Parker drew himself up and turned away from the window to look at his family. "I think I know what the problem is," he said confidently. "Gruff has lived with wolves for so long he doesn't know the difference between animals and people. Every shadow makes him jump."

"He'll get used to us," said Kim. "He already knows lots of things he didn't know when the hunters brought him out of the woods this morning. He just needs a little time."

Mr. Parker shook his head gravely. "No, I think the best way for Gruff to learn about humans and become a normal human boy is to plunge right in."

Kim and Paul looked at each other and at me, mystified.

"We're all new here in Fox Hollow," said Mr. Parker, speaking slowly so I would understand. "Wolfe Industries, a fine company, built the town and moved all the people here only two weeks ago. So you see, Gruff, none of us knows anyone else very well. The best thing for you would be to join in with all the other kids right away."

Then Mr. Parker spoke a word that sent chills up my spine. "School!" he said in a booming voice. "You will go to school as soon as we can arrange it."

Chapter 4

Mrs. Parker shooed Paul and Kim off to bed.

"Would it help you sleep if I left the light on, Gruff?" she asked.

At least that's what I thought she said. But how could anyone sleep better in the light? Dark was for sleeping. It wasn't night I was afraid of, but flesh-eating monsters.

As soon as everyone was gone I got into bed. But it wasn't like sleeping on the floor of my wolf pack's den. The bed surface was soft. I kept feeling like I was falling.

And it was lonely, curling up by myself. I was used to having all the warm wolf bodies tucked in around me. I missed Wolfmother and Thornclaw, my wolffather. And I missed my brother Sharpfang and especially the cuddly cubs.

I wondered where the wolves were now. The hunters from the town had chased them off and they could never go back to our old den. I wondered if they had found a new one yet.

Finally I got down off the bed and stretched out on the floor, pulling the blanket over my head. It wasn't the cozy wolf den but it was a little better.

I almost fell asleep. Then just as I started to nod off, something whispered and rustled outside under my window.

The werewolves were back!

I jumped up and went to the window. But there was nothing there. Nothing I could see, anyway.

After a while I gave up looking. I crawled under the bed with my blanket. The little space felt more like a den, and if the werewolves came through the window, maybe they wouldn't find me.

Chapter 5

It took almost two weeks for the Parkers to get me into school. I spent the time trying to learn to be a human boy — eating strange foods and watching the flickering box they called a *TV* to see how humans lived. The TV filled me with questions but it helped me a lot with my English.

Then one evening Mrs. Parker announced that Social Services had been unable to locate my parents and that I could stay with the Parkers, if that was all right with me. Was it! They could see from the grin on my face that it was fine with me.

But my grin faded fast when Mr. Parker said that now everything was set for me to go to school and I could start the next day. Up until now I had stayed indoors mostly, afraid to meet the townspeople who blamed me for the night the werewolves had almost stolen a little human baby. They didn't believe in werewolves and nothing could convince them that my wolf family wasn't to blame.

Also, even though I could understand more English from watching the TV, I still couldn't talk very well. I was curious about school but it was a mystery and it worried me that Paul didn't like it very much. He was always moaning about how lucky I was to get to stay home all day. Still, all the kids went to school. It was something human kids did. Maybe going to school would make me more human.

Mrs. Parker sent me to bed early, saying I should get a good night's sleep before my first day of school. I dragged myself upstairs but it was a long time before I fell asleep. In fact, I was sure I wouldn't sleep at all.

But the next thing I knew sunlight was streaming in and someone was banging on my door.

"Gruff! You awake?" It was Paul.

I scrambled out from under the bed. "Yes," I said, my voice coming out like a croak.

The door opened and Paul threw something on the bed. "Here's some clothes for school. Hurry! Mom always makes us eat breakfast before we go."

Even though I was now used to wearing jeans and T-shirts, it took me a while to figure out these new school clothes. In the woods I wore deerskins to protect me from the rain and cold. When I was little, Wolfmother chewed the hides for me to make them soft. When I got old enough to do it myself I figured out ways to hold the deerskins together with long pieces of dried deer sinew.

These school clothes were completely different. And not very comfortable. But finally I got them on me and went downstairs.

"Gruff! We're in the kitchen," yelled Paul.

He and Kim were already eating. They looked up when I appeared in the door. White liquid spurted out of Kim's mouth as she looked at me, her eyes crinkling. "M-milk," I said to myself, practicing English. Paul burst out laughing, spraying brown goo across the table.

"What's so funny?" asked Mrs. Parker, turning around with a glass in her hand. Her eyes widened. "Oh."

She frowned at Paul and Kim as she came toward me. "Here, Gruff, let me help you with that shirt. You've got it on backward. And you two," she said to the other kids, "clean up that mess. You ought to know better than to be laughing at people."

She smiled warmly as she helped me get the shirt turned around. It was much more comfortable that way. "Don't mind them, Gruff. I think you're very brave."

"Now," she went on, doing something to the top of my shirt, "you have to learn about buttons. I'll do the top two and you do the rest, okay?"

It was hard fitting the little round knobs into the narrow holes. I wondered why the humans would make shirts with buttons when they already had T-shirts. But finally I had it done.

"Excellent," said Mrs. Parker. "I'll just give your hair a little trim and you'll look quite respectable for your first day at school."

My neck felt strange and naked when she was done cutting my hair.

Acting like a human was hard. And the worst part of my day hadn't even started yet.

Chapter 6

Paul and Kim and I walked to school together. As we got close to the big square building I could hear the noise of kids running and yelling and shouting.

Breakfast cereal congealed in my stomach.

"Don't be scared," said Kim. "Everybody's pretty nice here." She made a face. "Well, maybe not everybody. But most people."

"I'll watch out for you," said Paul. "Just stick close to me."

But I wasn't really scared. Nervous, maybe, but mostly excited. I'd learned that school was something all kids did and there were no grown-ups, except for something called *teachers*, whatever they were.

True, these kids could do a lot of things I didn't know about. But my wolf family was always doing things I couldn't do and I'd been happy with them.

But now I was with creatures like me — humans. I missed my wolf family terribly but I knew I'd never be a wolf. And here I didn't need to have a super sense of smell or to run with the pack to find my food. Already I'd learned how to use a fork and a spoon and how to wear clothes. I was a human.

It seemed to me the only hard thing I had to learn was talking. Humans were really good at that and used it for everything.

But before I was ready we were in the school yard and there were kids surging and pushing all around me.

I heard whispers. "It's the wolf-boy! What's he doing here?"

"Wow, he looks almost normal."

"No, he doesn't. He's got a wild look in his eye."

"I wonder if he has a name."

"Go ask him. I dare you!"

It got weirdly quiet. Kids stopped yelling and playing to stare at me. Not knowing what else to do, I kept moving, my eyes darting around, afraid to look at anyone.

Then someone shouted, "Hey, wolf-boy! What'd you have for breakfast — chopped baby?"

The crowd of kids laughed like it was the best joke they'd ever heard. Their laughter sounded mean, cruel.

Suddenly I realized I'd lost Paul and Kim somewhere in the crowd. I was all alone!

Somebody started barking and a bunch of other kids joined in.

"RUFF, RUFF . . ."

"WOOF, WOOF . . ."

"AOOOH, AOOOH!"

I wanted to cover my ears and slink away but I didn't dare show how scared I felt. My wolf family had taught me that. Turn tail and everybody chases you. They can't help it.

Stand tall and sometimes it works.

So I stood tall and glared at the kids who were barking. A couple of them stopped and one even turned away. But the others laughed even harder.

Then one boy pushed through the crowd around me. He was a big kid with spiky blond hair and a nasty expression.

He came up close. "Hey, wolf-boy," he said, sneering down at me. "What do you want here? We don't need you."

I swallowed hard. Even if I had the words I wouldn't know what to say. I hoped he wouldn't notice I was shaking.

"What's the matter, wolf-boy, cat got your tongue?" He squinted at me, pushing his face so close to mine our noses were almost touching. I just stood there frozen, not moving an inch.

"He can't talk!" someone yelled while I was still trying to figure out how a cat could have my tongue — anyone could see there were no cats here.

"That's right, you can't talk," said the big kid, raising his voice for the crowd of kids. "But I'll bet you can fight."

Suddenly he reached out and shoved me. Taken by surprise, I stumbled backward. The crowd of kids moved back, making a circle around us.

Some of them started chanting. "Come on, Big Rick! Show him, Rick! Hit him, Rick!"

"Get 'em up, wolf-boy," said Big Rick. "I know all about you, you weirdo. I'm going to mop the floor with you. You think you can come here and make trouble, you're wrong. You can fool some of the grown-ups but not me. I know what you are."

Fear shot through me. What did he mean? How could he know about me? Nobody knew my horrible secret except my wolf family, and they weren't telling.

The werewolves! They knew — could this boy be one of them?

"Stop it, Rick, stop! Let me through!"

It was Paul. I turned to see him break away from two boys who were holding him.

I felt a rush of relief. My friend was going to help me!

Then something hard smashed me in the face. Pain exploded along my cheekbone.

I was so surprised I just stood there, my hand to my face.

I felt like I'd run into a tree. But it was just Rick's fist. He had hit me when I wasn't looking.

"Come on, wolf-boy," he taunted. "You chicken?"

Paul appeared by my side. "Leave him alone, Rick," said Paul, his chest heaving with exertion. "He hasn't done anything to you."

"Beat it, squirt," said Big Rick and shoved Paul so hard he fell down.

Inside me, something snapped. He had no reason to hit Paul!

Suddenly I knew I was going to fight this bully and beat him. He had never wrestled with Sharpfang, my wolfbrother. Sharpfang was all muscle and teeth. Rick was all mouth.

I went into a fighting crouch and snarled at him from deep in my throat. It was a good deep menacing snarl but I wasn't prepared for what happened next.

Rick dropped his hands and backed off, a look of fear and horror on his face.

Then I noticed he wasn't looking at me. He was looking behind me.

Something heavy fell on my shoulder. Claws dug into my flesh.

And behind me something snarled.

Chapter 7

I spun around.

Red eyes burned into mine. "Caught!"

At first I thought a werewolf had grabbed me in broad daylight! Terrified, I couldn't have pulled away even if the grip on my shoulder wasn't so tight.

Then I realized it wasn't a werewolf after all — just a man with gray hair sprouting out of his ears and bloodshot eyes. But the way he was looking at me was still scary.

A ripple went through the kids behind me. "The principal!" They whispered in frightened voices. "Mr. Clawson is here!"

Mr. Clawson ignored everyone but me.

"I knew there'd be trouble with you," he said through clenched teeth. "School hasn't even started yet and already you're fighting."

Paul spoke up. "But, Mr. Clawson," he said, "Gruff didn't do anything. It was Rick who started it."

Mr. Clawson scowled at him. "When I want your opinion, Paul Parker, I'll ask for it. We've never had a problem with fighting in this school. And we've never had a wolf-boy either."

A bell rang and all the kids started to line up. I tried to move off with Paul but Mr. Clawson tightened his grip again. "I want to speak to you in my office. And then we'll decide what to do with you."

Mr. Clawson marched me across the school yard and through a side door. We turned into a room where a woman sat tapping at a machine on her desk. She looked up and smiled.

It was a friendly smile, like she was pleased to see me. I started to relax a little but Mr. Clawson marched past her like she wasn't there. Her smile wobbled as if a thundercloud had passed.

At the back of this room there was another door. Mr. Clawson opened it and pushed me inside. Then he pulled the door shut, leaving me alone.

The room was dark. There was a window but the shade was pulled down. The things in the room seemed to watch me. And they didn't like what they saw.

Nothing in the Parker house had prepared me for this room. At the Parkers' everything was new and shiny, mysterious maybe, but not scary. Mr. Clawson's things were old, older than I could even imagine. And they seemed to radiate a feeling of menace.

On a big wooden desk with clawed feet a strange battered thing shaped like a metal head stared blindly at me, with slits where the eyes should be. Beside it was another weird object with three big screws. I shuddered and backed away.

And the walls! At the Parkers' house the walls were covered with pretty pictures of the outdoors. But instead of pictures Mr. Clawson had put up evil-looking weapons. In the center of the wall hung a big club with sharp metal spikes sticking out all over the end. This club had brown stains on the spikes and what looked like bits of hair. I leaned closer. It *was* hair!

Behind me the door opened. I jumped.

"Now we won't be disturbed with any interruptions," said Mr. Clawson, shutting the door firmly behind him. He leaned against it, studying me. There was a smile on his face, but it was a strange kind of smile. His eyes were as cold and gray as river pebbles.

"I see you've been admiring my collection of medieval weapons," he said in a cold voice. "Unfortunately, I've never had a chance to use any of them — yet."

He moved to the desk and I flinched as he brushed past me. "Do you know what this is?"

he asked, resting his hand gently on the small metal object with the screws. "Some principals keep pencil sharpeners on their desks," he said with a growly chuckle. "But this is no pencil sharpener. It's something much more useful. Can you guess what it is? No? It's a thumb-screw. Ingenious device and so simple. Let me show you how it works."

He opened a drawer in his desk and took out a small bowl of plump purple grapes. He put two of them in the shallow spaces between the screws, then began to turn two of the screws. As they turned, metal plates slowly squished the grapes until — *PLOP!* — they burst, spewing reddish pulp all over the polished desk.

Mr. Clawson sat back and laughed. "Imagine what that could do to a man's — or a boy's — thumbs. Clever, isn't it?"

I nodded, putting my hands behind my back. My chest tightened.

"And this," said Mr. Clawson cheerily, laying his thick hand on the top of the metal thing that was shaped like a head. "This is armor. A helmet. It protected a man's head from arrows and stones. You can see the dents," he said, signaling me to come closer.

My legs felt wooden. Stiffly I approached the desk.

"It's too small for me but perhaps you'd like to try it on." Mr. Clawson's eyes gleamed.

I shook my head no and backed away.

Mr. Clawson frowned. "Of course you would. Any normal boy would."

He picked up the head and came at me. There was no place for me to go. Numbly I stood there while he raised the thing over my head and then lowered it over my face.

It was dark. I couldn't see a thing. I couldn't breathe.

"Yes," said Mr. Clawson. "That's better." He chuckled to himself and I heard him move away.

Panicky, my breath was hot against my face. I needed air. I pushed up on the metal around my neck but couldn't get it off. It was stuck!

I was suffocating.

Chapter 8

I pushed harder at the suffocating helmet, my heart fluttering. It slid an inch and I could breath again.

I could also see a narrow slice of the room through the eye slit.

Mr. Clawson was taking the spiky club with the hair stuck on it down from the wall. "This club is called a mace," he said calmly. "A blow to the head from one of these could be pretty nasty, even with armor."

He bounced the club in his hand, careful not to hit himself with the spikes, and looked at me, narrowing his eyes.

"This is a nice town," he said. "A new town, built around a fine company — Wolfe Industries, not that you'd know anything about that. And this is a brand-new school. It's my school and I'm going to run it the way I please, understand?"

I nodded, feeling the metal armor bang the back of my head. I couldn't take my eyes off the club, bouncing against his hand.

"You're a troublemaker and you don't belong here."

My face was hot. I felt like I was going to

throw up inside the helmet. My hands were clammy with sweat.

"And no one would miss you if you just disappeared, would they?" Mr. Clawson took a step toward me, hefting the club and smiling a secret smile.

Paul would, I wanted to shout. Kim would! And Mr. and Mrs. Parker. But I couldn't speak. I was choking.

"Oh, the Parkers might experience a pang of regret," Mr. Clawson sneered. "But they'd understand. The wild wolf-boy couldn't handle his first day of school and ran off back to the swamp. Perfectly understandable, don't you agree?"

Mr. Clawson took another step toward me, then another. Slowly he raised the club. "No one will question it if you disappear."

I tried to cry out but my voice was muffled inside the helmet.

Mr. Clawson showed his long, yellowish teeth in a cruel smile. "I sent my secretary on an errand," he said. "There's no one in this part of the building but you and me."

He came closer. I couldn't see his face anymore through the eye slit. All I could see was his big broad chest and the arm raising the club over my head.

I backed away and bumped against the door. The door! I had to get out! Quickly I scrabbled for the doorknob behind me. I couldn't find it!

Ducking sideways, I felt frantically for the knob. At last, there it was.

I gripped the knob but it wouldn't turn! My hands were too slick with sweat. They slipped right off.

And then it was too late. My time was up.

Mr. Clawson grunted with effort as he brought his arm back for a better swing.

I threw myself sideways but there was no room to escape the blow.

I heard a *whoosh!* of air, a terrible banging, ringing noise, and then nothing.

Nothing but darkness blacker than night.

Chapter 9

Blood hammered in my head, making a dull thudding noise in the blackness surrounding me.

Something scraped hard against my ear.

"OW!"

I was jerked to my feet.

Panic leaped in my chest.

My ear felt like it was being sawed off.

Suddenly light flashed into my eyes, blinding me with brightness. A rush of cool air blew over my face. The helmet was off my head.

I gulped in air and a shadow passed over me. My eyes cleared. I jumped and let out a yelp of fear.

Mr. Clawson's face was an inch from mine. His eyes were peering intently at me. He grunted.

"You certainly are a jumpy boy," he said with a satisfied grin. He put the old armor helmet back on his desk and straightened, looking down on me from a great height.

"And now you've had your first lesson." Mr. Clawson put his hands on his hips. "Which is that I run things and I know how to deal with troublemakers, right?"

I nodded, swallowing nervously.

Without taking his eyes off me, Mr. Clawson reached into his desk and pulled out a sheet of paper. He glanced at it briefly. "I'm going to put you in Miss Possum's class with Paul Parker. For the time being."

Miserable and frightened as I was, I felt a surge of hope.

Mr. Clawson noticed. He narrowed his eyes. "I still think you belong in a special school for creatures like you. A place where they have locks on the cages" — he grinned slyly — "I mean the doors."

I blinked, feeling the little warm spot of hope grow cold.

"But," Mr. Clawson raised his voice, "against my better judgment I've decided to give you a chance to prove you can make it with normal kids. If not — "

Mr. Clawson broke off suddenly and stared at his office door. The doorknob was turning.

Mr. Clawson's face turned purple.

His eyes began to bug out.

He bared his teeth and I could have sworn they were sharper and yellower.

In one long stride he reached the door and yanked it open.

Chapter 10

"Oh!"

Paul stumbled into the office as the door jerked open. He almost fell as he let go of the doorknob.

"Yes, Paul?" asked Mr. Clawson in a menacing voice.

"Miss Possum asked me to see if Gruff was ready to come to class yet," Paul answered, his voice trembling slightly.

"I suppose so," Mr. Clawson said reluctantly, shooting me one last, dark look. "But I'll be keeping my eye on you, wolf-boy."

The halls of the school were deserted. I was so relieved to escape from the principal's office that I hardly noticed at first. Then it started to worry me. Our footsteps echoed loudly in the stillness.

"Where kids?" I asked, struggling to remember the right words.

"Class has started," said Paul. "Everyone's in their classrooms. Come on, Gruff, we better hurry."

He stopped at a door, looked in the window and motioned me to look, too. "That's our class," he said.

I looked in and saw rows of kids sitting motionless. None of them talked or smiled or moved. They just stared straight ahead at a lady who stood up in front and talked at them.

My pulse started to race. Mr. Clawson ran this place! He had found some way to take over the minds of children. What was he planning?

"What we do?" I asked Paul. "How we save them?"

"Huh?" Paul shook his head at me. "Sometimes you don't make any sense at all, Gruff. Come on, we've got to go in. Just stick with me and I'll show you what to do."

Paul opened the door.

"No, Paul!"

Too late. He was already inside. I had to follow. I couldn't leave him to rescue his friends alone. I hoped he had a plan.

Taking a shuddery breath, I stepped into the room.

Instantly, all eyes switched to me. The lady at the front of the room started to turn. I braced myself. I wouldn't let her take over my mind, no matter what!

"So, this is our new pupil," she said, clapping her hands together.

My knees began to tremble.

"His name is Gruff," said Paul. "Gruff, this is our teacher, Miss Possum."

She smiled at me. Miss Possum had rosy cheeks and very blue eyes. They crinkled when she smiled. She didn't look in the least dangerous.

The kids now began to fidget and whisper. I heard giggles that I knew were aimed at me.

"Pleased to have you here, Gruff. Do you have a last name?" asked Miss Possum in a very gentle and friendly voice.

"No last name," said Paul quickly. "Gruff doesn't speak English very well yet."

One of the kids yelled out. "Ask him to speak wolf. He can howl like anything!"

A bunch of kids burst out laughing. I decided I liked them better when they were just sitting there like brain-dead statues.

Miss Possum frowned. It didn't look very threatening. "Quiet, class," she said mildly. "Gruff is new here and we all want to show him how pleased we are to have him in class."

She turned back to me. "We're having language arts class now, Gruff, and this is the book we're reading."

She handed me a big heavy book. I opened it but there were no pictures, just long lines of black squiggles. I turned the book around but the black marks still didn't look like anything. I knew they were words — Kim had shown me words in some of her old picture books — but in this book there were so many and they were so small. I started to feel panicky.

Then a burst of loud laughter startled me. I looked up in surprise.

Miss Possum was staring at me wide-eyed.

Some of the kids were pointing and laughing so hard they were falling out of their seats. "GRRRUFFF!" shouted someone from the back of the room and everyone laughed harder.

I wanted to disappear through the floor.

Miss Possum frowned at the class and turned the book around in my hands. But the kids kept laughing. For some reason it was funny to them that I didn't know how to use the book. And the longer I stood there wanting to sink through the floor, the harder they laughed.

So I started laughing myself. I turned the book upside down again, shrugging my shoulders. I laughed harder.

I laughed so hard I drowned out the other kids. And somehow that made it better. If I could laugh at myself then it didn't sting so much when they did it.

Then I got a real shock. I looked out at all

those mocking faces and saw that lots of them were grinning at me — in a friendly, interested way. And Paul was smiling, too, like somehow everything was okay now.

I started to feel like I might even fit in — in a year or so.

But just as I was starting to breathe again I saw a flash of movement outside the door.

My spine turned to ice. It couldn't be!

I saw it again. A snarling face, covered with straggly hair, and sharp, dripping fangs.

A werewolf!

Here in the school! It was after the kids. We must have attracted it by making so much noise.

I couldn't let it get away.

Growling deep in my throat, I leaped for the door.

Chapter 11

I opened the door and threw myself at the slobbering monster.

But as I lunged, my fighting snarl changed to a whimper.

I stopped so short my sneakers left rubber tracks on the floor.

There was no werewolf lurking outside the classroom. Again, I had mistaken the school principal for a monster.

"What is the meaning of this?" demanded Mr. Clawson furiously, backing away from me.

It was lucky I still couldn't speak properly. The true explanation would have sent Mr. Clawson into an even worse rage.

"It must have startled him to see a face in the window," said Miss Possum, hurrying to stand beside me. "I'm afraid the poor boy still isn't used to so many people."

I nodded eagerly. "Yes, Mr. Claw-son," I said. "I sorry."

"Poor boy! Sorry!" Mr. Clawson sneered. "He's nothing but a wild animal."

No one in the class laughed. It was so quiet I could feel how glad the other kids were not to be standing in my shoes.

"We have a long road ahead of us with this one, Miss Possum," said the principal, stroking his lip. I could tell he was trying to think of a really good punishment.

"Oh, I don't know," said Miss Possum with a little fluttery laugh. "He just needs a little time and guidance."

Mr. Clawson nodded as if he was agreeing with her. He pointed a finger at me. "Detention!" he announced in a voice of doom.

Miss Possum looked sad. Behind me I felt the kids get even quieter. I started to shake with fear. What was this horrible thing called *detention*?

Mr. Clawson turned on his heel and walked out.

I couldn't fix my mind on anything for the rest of the morning. I just kept worrying about what Mr. Clawson had said. What was *detention*? What would it do to me?

At lunch Paul tried to explain it to me. "It means you have to stay after school for half an hour."

I nodded. "And what happen?"

"Happen? Nothing," said Paul. "That's it. Nobody likes to stay after school when everybody else is out playing. And Mr. Clawson doesn't let you do homework or anything. You have to just sit so it seems to take forever."

Sit for half an hour? That was all? I was so relieved my appetite came back. I had just picked up my sandwich and opened my mouth to take a bite when —

PLOP!

Something wet and gooey smacked me right in the face. I was so startled I forgot to close my mouth. Soft lumpy stuff dripped onto my tongue. It wasn't bad. Tasted pretty good in fact.

Paul jumped out of his chair and it fell with a crash. "Come on, Gruff, we've got to get out of here!" he yelled, pulling at my arm.

As I leaped up in alarm a round piece of pink meat smeared with yellow bounced off my shirt, leaving a trail of ooze.

I didn't like that. I caught the meat before it hit the ground and pulled my arm back, looking around to see who had thrown it.

"No, Gruff!" shouted Paul. "Come on."

I dropped the meat and followed him. Behind me someone yelled "Food fight!"

When we reached the cafeteria door I looked back. Gobs and chunks were flying. A girl with a piece of wadded bread stuck in her hair rubbed a handful of brown glop into a boy's face. Another kid was covered in the red goo they call "ketchup."

Food fighting looked like a lot of fun. My wolf family never did anything like this. Oh, sometimes the cubs scrapped over a piece of meat but basically wolves don't play with their food. My fingers itched to throw something. I had good aim. I knew I'd be good at this game and I could even eat what landed on me!

"Franks and beans," said Paul, making a face. "What a mess."

"Yes," I said enthusiastically. "Big mess. Why we leave?"

Paul gave me a disgusted look. "Do you want to get blamed for this, too? Clawson has it in for you. You'd get detention for a week if he caught you throwing food."

I shrugged. Detention didn't seem so bad if it just meant staying after school for a while.

Looking at the kids laughing and hurling food and covered with bits and pieces of it, I wished I was with them. I licked at a lump of brown stuff stuck at the corner of my mouth. Detention would be worth it.

But then, as teachers came running to break up the food fight, I felt a twinge of uncertainty. Paul was right. Mr. Clawson didn't like me.

I remembered the sudden gleam in his eye when he snarled, "Detention!"

I shivered remembering how he had said no one would miss me if I disappeared.

Mr. Clawson was planning something special for me.

And he was the only one who was going to enjoy it.

Chapter 12

Paul had a mournful look on his face when he said good-bye at the end of school. "See you at home," he said, but I could tell he didn't believe it.

I turned around and started trudging for Mr. Clawson's office. My feet felt like they were made of lead. My stomach, too.

"Not trying to sneak off, were you boy?"

Startled, I looked up. Mr. Clawson was standing outside his office, waiting for me.

Unable to speak, I shook my head.

"Good." He rubbed his hands together. "This way," he cackled. "We don't want to be disturbed."

He led the way to a metal door painted green. Through the door were stairs leading down.

The door clanged firmly behind us and shut out all the little noises of the closing school — kids running, teachers chatting, cars and buses leaving. Even if I screamed nobody would hear me.

Our footsteps echoed on the stairs, the only noise. Mr. Clawson didn't say a word. But he was close behind me.

Down and down we went, deep below the

school. I could feel the earth pressing on the walls around us.

Dust hung in the air and there were already big spiderwebs in the corners even though the building was almost new. Big green pipes ran along the walls.

Something clanked and gurgled ahead of us and I jumped in fear.

Mr. Clawson chuckled quietly but he still didn't say anything.

We passed a room where the gurgling noise was coming from. Inside, a huge machine hummed and threw off heat.

We turned a corner. The light grew dimmer.

I didn't think this was where the other kids came for detention. Probably most kids didn't even know this creepy basement existed. Nobody would ever think to look for me here.

"Here we are," said Mr. Clawson heartily.

We stopped before a heavy green door.

A fat brown spider was busy building a web that attached to the doorknob. The startled spider made the mistake of running across Mr. Clawson's hand when he reached for the knob and opened the door.

"Gotcha, you little beast!" Smiling, the principal crushed the spider in his fist and dropped the crumpled body to the floor.

"You're gonna love it in here, wolf-boy," Mr. Clawson growled.

Beyond the door was nothing but darkness.

He pressed a switch near the door and light flooded a small, windowless room. It was empty except for a wooden table and a couple of chairs.

"Wait in here," said Mr. Clawson, shoving me into the room. "I'll be right back."

He hurriedly backed out and shut the heavy metal door behind him. I heard his footsteps heading back the way we'd come and then — nothing.

I strained my ears for a sound of life outside. Some kids playing, maybe, or a janitor moving desks around. But no sound reached me in this faraway basement room.

Sitting down at the table, I sighed and waited. I wanted to think about all the new things that had happened today but my mind kept jumping back to thoughts of Mr. Clawson. I couldn't stop worrying.

Where was he? What was he doing? Why did he hate me?

I couldn't tell how much time had passed. It seemed like I had been in that room for hours.

Maybe this was my whole punishment. Maybe nothing else would happen and soon

Mr. Clawson would come and tell me to go home.

The silence began to press on my ears. It felt like a heavy wet blanket wrapping my head.

Maybe if I practiced my talking. "Hello," I said, trying to break up the quiet. "My n-name is G-Gruff. Wh-What is yours?"

But my voice was too loud. I tried it again in a whisper but even that was too loud. I was afraid I wouldn't hear Mr. Clawson when he came to let me out. It seemed important that the principal shouldn't hear me talking to myself.

CLICK!

What was that? I jumped up. It was right outside the door. But I hadn't heard anyone coming.

SNICK!

That noise! I'd heard it before. I'd heard it this morning when Mrs. Parker locked the front door.

No! I ran to the door and twisted the knob. It wouldn't turn. I was locked in! And no one but Mr. Clawson knew where I was.

"Help!" I yelled. "Help!"

I pressed my ear to the door and listened. No one answered. No one came.

But I heard whispering. Someone was out in

48

the hall. Who? Why didn't they answer me?

I couldn't make out what they were saying although I listened with all my might. I closed my eyes and concentrated. The whispering voices were coming closer. And closer.

They were right outside the door. Something gave a low, evil chuckle.

I jumped back from the door as if it were hot.

The hair on the back of my neck prickled.

I looked around me. There was no place to hide.

Then the lights went out.

I was plunged into utter darkness.

Chapter 13

I'd never been afraid of the dark, but this was different.

Deep underground in that spooky basement, no particle of light reached me. I stretched my eyes wide and saw nothing at all.

Claws scratched at the outside of the locked door.

I stumbled backward, knocking over a chair. The noise echoed in the black silence.

The whispers grew louder as if the thing outside the door was pressed up against it, its lips to the crack between door and wall.

I began to hear words.

"Keep the secret, little one! Remember the three nights of the full moon. Remember the wereing or die. Keep the secret and save yourself!"

There was a werewolf out there! The werewolves knew I was one of them. They knew I turned into a monster during the three nights of the full moon.

But I had hidden from them and I hadn't yet made my first kill. So I remained a boy the rest of the month. The werewolves were angry about that. Very angry. And unlike me, they could turn into monsters whenever they chose.

I scuttled into a corner and pressed myself into the wall. Claws raked at the door and then began to scratch around the lock.

"Remember who you are! Save yourself!"

Panic bubbled through my blood, jumping and twitching under my skin.

Had Mr. Clawson left me here for the were-wolves to find?

Claws scratched at the lock.

Would they tear me to pieces? Or would they carry me off to live with them until the next full moon?

SNAP!

They'd gotten the lock open!

I threw myself toward where I thought the table was. If I could get hold of a chair maybe I could fend them off for a few minutes.

I was so scared I couldn't think past the next minute when the monsters would be inside the room. Inside with me, in the dark where I couldn't see them.

My fingers grasped the leg of a chair. I wouldn't let them take me.

I heard the doorknob turn.

The door began to creak.

I scrambled to my feet, holding the chair above my head. I was ready to crash it down on the first werewolf through the door.

Slowly the door swung open.

Chapter 14

Light flashed into my eyes.

My arm jerked and the chair fell with a thunderous clatter.

A figure slipped through the door into the room.

"Gruff! What are you doing?"

It was Miss Possum. She stared at me in amazement.

"D-d-detention," I stuttered. My eyes darted to the hallway behind her. Where were the werewolves?

"Detention? Here?" She looked surpised. "Well, Mr. Clawson must have forgotten about you," said Miss Possum. "It's a good thing I came down for some supplies. And then I heard noises down this way."

She paused and peered back into the hallway, as if she'd missed something. "Strange," she said, wrinkling her nose thoughtfully. "It sounded like an animal. I thought a cat might have gotten trapped down here."

I inched past her and peered out the door. There was no sign of the werewolves. Could I have imagined the whole thing? Could it have been a cat, like Miss Possum thought?

"N-noises. Yes," I said in a shaky voice. "Mr. Clawson has dog, maybe, or cat?"

"Heavens, no," said Miss Possum. "Mr. Clawson doesn't have a dog. He doesn't care for animals of any kind." She touched my elbow and smiled kindly. "I'm sure you're anxious to get out of here," she said, steering me toward the door. "Why don't we go?"

I peered into the shadows down the hall. Nothing moved.

Tension began to flow out of my muscles. The darkness and the silence had spooked me, I thought. There never had been anything down here.

Then my eye caught sight of something on the floor. Without thinking I stooped and picked it up. A cold invisible finger ran down my spine.

"What's that, Gruff?"

Reluctantly, I opened my hand and showed it to her.

"Oh," she cried. "Fur! I knew I heard a cat scratching. We've got to find it, Gruff. Will you help me? It'll starve down here."

All my fear and dread came rushing back. No, I wanted to yell, it's not a cat! It's a monster that probably eats nice teachers for an afternoon snack!

But Miss Possum was already hurrying down the hall making little "psst, psst" noises and calling out "Here, kitty, here, kitty."

I rushed after her but she disappeared around a corner before I could catch up.

"Goodness, it's dark here!" Her voice came from deep in the shadows. "Gruff, could you get the light? The switch must be on the wall in that hallway, there's no switch here —

"AAEEEEK! AAAA! EEEE!"

Miss Possum's scream stood my hair on end. I dashed after her, my heart in my throat, forgetting all about the light switch.

CRASH! THUD!

The werewolves had got her!

Chapter 15

I skidded around the corner.

The hallway was dark but faint light filtered in behind me.

I could see Miss Possum struggling with something big. It was hard to see in the shadows, but I was pretty sure it had long arms and a shaggy head filled with sharp teeth. Miss Possum never stood a chance.

Her screams had stopped. All that came from her were little grunts and gasps.

She must be badly hurt already!

Snarling, I leaped onto the back of the werewolf.

OOF!

Something hard and pointed hit me in the stomach. The thing pulled away from me. Off balance, I went crashing to the floor.

Heavy objects fell all around me. I scrambled clear, trying to find the monster.

"Stop, Gruff, stop!" Miss Possum pulled on my arm. "You're knocking these boxes everywhere. I only hope there's nothing breakable in them."

Boxes? I put my hand out and felt the corner of one. So that's what hit me in the stomach. I must have jumped right on it, fooled by the shadows.

"You not hurt?" I asked Miss Possum.

She laughed nervously. "A mouse ran over my foot and I screamed," she said. "When I jumped away, I hit this stack of boxes. I was trying to keep it from falling over."

I was too relieved to feel foolish. Now maybe Miss Possum would agree to get out of here. "Cat not starve," I said, grinning. "Eat mouse."

"Right," she said, with a nervous giggle. "Let's just get these boxes straightened up and get out of here. I'll tell Mr. Clawson about the cat and explain that I sent you home.

Outside the air was fresh and clean and sunlight sparkled in the trees. It felt so good I was ready to forget every single bad thing that had happened today.

Then Miss Possum said something that stopped me in my tracks.

My stomach churned with dread as again my world came crashing down around me.

Chapter 16

"We need to talk about your schooling, Gruff," said nice Miss Possum with a sad little frown. "It's not your fault you've never been to school, but I know you can't do the sixth-grade work."

I opened my mouth and shut it again. I was gasping like a fish.

Paul had told me that kids who couldn't read went to first grade. I'd seen the first graders. They were little kids. None of them stood any higher than my waist. If I had to go to first grade I couldn't bear it. How could I hold my head up around the kids my own age?

Miss Possum cocked her head and looked at me worriedly. "Well, never mind," she said, patting my shoulder. "I think the stress of your first day is enough for now. We'll wait and see how you're doing next week."

My heart leaped. Could I learn to read and write and talk in a week? I had to or else Miss Possum would send me to first grade.

I shuddered to think what that bully Rick would say if I was a first grader. And all the sixth graders would laugh like crazy.

I trudged toward the Parkers' house, head down.

"Hey, Gruff. Hey!" I looked up to see Paul running toward me across a field. He had a big glove on his hand. A bunch of other kids stood around the field, looking at a kid with a wooden club on his shoulder.

"Come play baseball with us," said Paul. "It'll be a good way to meet everybody."

Just then one of the kids threw something white at the boy with the club. He swung the club and *WHACK!* the white thing sailed high into the air.

Wow! My spirits seemed to fly up with it. I wondered if I could do that. It sure would be fun to try. I started running across the field with Paul and then I remembered that I had something more important to do.

"No," I said, thinking of Miss Possum. "I learn read."

Paul didn't understand. "School's over," he said. "Forget about it."

I was tempted. But I pictured myself standing in line with all the little first graders and Rick and all of Paul's friends jeering at me. I left Paul and ran the rest of the way to his family's house.

* * *

My head was spinning with all the alphabet sounds Kim was teaching me.

"Why have c?" I asked her. "Already have k sound and s sound. Not need c."

Kim sighed and scratched her head. "For one thing, you need it for words like 'church.'" She wrote down the word.

"What is church?" I asked.

Kim's shoulders slumped. "This teaching stuff is much harder than I expected," she said. "Anyway we're supposed to be doing letter sounds. We'll discuss church later. Now try and sound out this word."

But before she could write it, a voice called from downstairs. "Dinner," Mrs. Parker announced. "Kim, Paul, Gruff!"

My stomach growled. All this brain work had made me hungry. And the smells from the kitchen were wonderful. I jumped up instantly and bounded downstairs.

But where was everybody? I was the only one at the table.

Mrs. Parker came out of the kitchen carrying a steaming bowl. She looked surprised to see me. "Sit down, Gruff," she said, smiling. "It's nice to see one person in this house comes when I call. This family is very slow getting to the dinner table. Anyone would think they didn't like my cooking."

"Not like cooking!" I was shocked. "Smell is delicious."

Mrs. Parker beamed at me. "Thank you, Gruff."

She set the bowl down and turned away to go back into the kitchen. "I'll be right back. And everyone else should be down in a minute."

Meat smells rose into the air. My stomach growled again. I was starved. I knew I was expected to wait until the whole family sat down but it was very hard.

Finally Mr. Parker arrived and Mrs. Parker came back from the kitchen with a loaf of bread.

"What's for dinner, Carol?" asked Mr. Parker, sitting in his chair at the end of the table.

"Beef stew," said Mrs. Parker, sitting down at the other end.

She started ladling the food into bowls. The wonderful smell made my head swim with hunger. I was practically drooling.

I had to sit on my hands to keep from snatching up the bowl she put in front of me. But I still had to wait for Kim and Paul.

At last they showed up. "Smells good, Mom," said Paul, sliding into his seat.

"Not stew again," complained Kim. "Yuck!"

I stared at her in amazement and then looked at my bowl. Big chunks of meat and earthy-smelling vegetables. What could be better? My stomach growled. I didn't think I could stand to wait another second.

"We can't have spaghetti every night, Kim," said her mother. "Just eat what you can."

I watched Mrs. Parker for the signal to start eating. When she started eating, the rest of us could, too. At least that's how it always was with Wolfmother.

Finally Mrs. Parker finished dishing out the food. Then she took her napkin and spread it carefully in her lap.

Quickly I did the same. The meat smell was making me dizzy with hunger. I eyed the juicy chunks longingly.

Then Mrs. Parker looked around the table. "Everyone have what they need? Good."

At long last she broke off a piece of bread and dipped it in her stew. The signal! We could eat!

I buried my face in the bowl, filling my nose with the scent. Growling with pleasure, I grabbed the first chunk of meat with my teeth, feeling the juices spurt as I bit down. Mmmmm, good!

I lapped up the rich gravy and wolfed down the vegetables, chomping them together with the tender meat. It was so delicious I hardly remembered to chew.

Too soon, it was all gone. I looked up, wondering if there was more.

A shock of alarm jolted through me. The whole family was staring at me.

"Wow," said Paul. "Cool!"

But no one else seemed to think so.

I wanted to crawl under the table in embarrassment. I'd been so overcome by the delicious smell and all the waiting, I'd completely forgotten about forks. Humans had such complicated eating habits and they were very particular about them.

"Gross," said Kim, looking disgusted. "No offense, Gruff, but only dogs eat like that. And wolves, I guess. People use forks."

Suddenly I was aware of the grease glistening on my face. I wiped at it with my fingers, wondering what would happen to me now.

"Use your napkin to wipe your face, Gruff," said Mrs. Parker gently. "And don't mind Kim. It's true that's not the way we eat but we don't expect you to learn all our ways all at once." She broke into a wide grin. "Besides, I don't think I've ever seen anyone enjoy a bowl of my stew quite so much."

It was so hard learning all the rules of being a human.

Would I ever get it right?

What horrible mistake would I make next?

Chapter 17

That night I woke to moonlight in my face. Startled, I sat up quickly, my heart racing. Something had woken me from a sound sleep.

The moonlight? But the moonlight was faint. It was only a quarter moon and the light was barely enough to outline the shapes of furniture in my room. Surely that hadn't awakened me. And everything was quiet. Even the breeze barely stirred the curtains at my window.

So what had snapped me out of a deep sleep? What was it that made my heart race with fright?

My eye kept going to the dark outline of the window. Something was out there.

I didn't want to get up and look but I had to. A strange urgency told me to hurry. I pushed off the bedclothes and ran to the window.

At first I didn't see anything. The street was quiet. The backyard was in deep shadow, the moonlight showing only in dim patches through the trees.

Then a figure moved. Dressed in white, it looked like a ghost flitting from shadow to shadow. I stared harder, trying to make out who — or what — it was.

But it disappeared behind a tree and I saw nothing. Had I imagined it? It was so dark and so late. Perhaps all I'd seen was a piece of paper blowing in the breeze.

No — there it was again! Moving slowly, almost floating, the white figure came out of the shadows. Moonlight touched its head and it looked up.

It wasn't a ghost! It was Kim!

I opened my mouth to shout her name out the window but a worried feeling stopped me. It seemed important to be quiet, although I didn't know why.

Kim vanished into another dark pool of shadow and then reappeared, farther away. There was a strange, jerky motion to the way she was moving.

And she was heading for the woods!

Again I started to call out and again I stopped myself.

Something might hear me.

And it wouldn't be Kim.

Kim was walking into the swamp. And she looked like the living dead.

Chapter 18

I had to stop Kim from disappearing into the woods!

Without even pausing to put on my sneakers I flew out of my room and down the stairs.

I had a bad moment when I got to the kitchen and saw the back door standing partway open. Anything could have gotten in. But there was no time to worry about that now. I slipped out the door and shut it behind me.

But where was Kim? I dashed across the yard and down toward the woods where I had last seen her. There was no sign of her.

Could she have reached the woods already? Was she heading for the swamp?

Uncertain which way to go, afraid to cry out, I looked around, my eyes darting every which way. But it was so dark I couldn't see two feet in front of me. Dread curled in a cold ball in my stomach as the seconds ticked by. What if I couldn't find Kim?

I hurried toward the next clump of trees. She wasn't there. I was getting very close to the woods and the trees were getting thicker. No moonlight pierced the thick leaves above me.

The night was so black I stubbed my toe on a

rock sticking up out of the ground. I stifled a cry, wishing I had my werewolf powers now.

During the three nights of the full moon I had been a hideous monster. But I had learned how powerful and superior it felt to be a werewolf. As a monster I could see in the dark clear as day. I could smell living creatures wherever they hid from me, whether it was deep in the ground or high in a tree.

A werewolf could find Kim in a second.

The thought made my skin crawl. And then I heard a sound that turned me to stone. Something rustling in the dead leaves on the ground. It was the furtive noise of a big creature prowling the woods.

My heart hammered against my ribs. It was coming closer. A whiff of something foul and dead filled my nostrils. Whatever was out there, it wasn't human.

A twig cracked behind me. I jumped, my skin tingling all over, and whipped around. But all I could see was darkness everywhere.

I whipped around again as I heard a growl at my back. My eyes strained to see. A black shape moved. The growl came again, low and rumbling, sounding amused.

"Grrrrrrrrrrrr."

I knew that sound. The werewolf growl! I felt

its eyes on me, watching me. My neck prickled as I sensed it staring, coming almost silently closer.

It was coming to get me.

My muscles tensed.

"Hehehehegrrrrrrr."

It was growling and laughing and smacking its jaws together in a frenzy of anticipation.

I ran.

But not quick enough. Its grip was strong enough to pull my shoulder out of its socket. Claws raked my arm.

I was caught.

Chapter 19

I flailed around, struggling to free myself from the creature. My hand grabbed something hard and rough.

A tree branch!

It was only a tree branch that had snagged me. Quickly I wrenched my pajama top free and raced toward the Parkers' backyard. Twigs whipped across my face as I fled blindly out of the trees.

I heard heavy breathing over my shoulder.

But where was Kim? If the creature didn't catch me, it would take out its rage on Kim. I had to do something to save her, but what?

The only thing I could do was scream once I got close enough to the house. If I could wake the family, maybe they could save Kim. Maybe they could even save me.

Blindly I ran, my face stinging. I felt the creature gaining on me but I couldn't hear it over the ragged sound of my own harsh breathing. Ahead of me, lawn swept up to the house and faint moonlight glinted off the windows.

I looked longingly at the house.

Suddenly, out of the shadows, a floating

shape darted right in front of me. I tried to swerve but it was too close.

"Ooomph!"

I smacked into something smaller and slighter than me, knocking it to the ground.

"Kim!"

It was Kim I had smashed into. She sat up slowly, shaking her head as if to clear it.

"Where am I?" she asked dreamily, looking around the backyard with a puzzled look on her face. "How did I get here?"

"Outside. You sleepw-walk," I said, glancing nervously over my shoulder. But I no longer sensed the werewolf behind me. It had moved off, not willing to attack both of us for some reason.

Kim nodded, getting slowly to her feet. "That's right," she said. "I remember now, I was sleeping." She looked into my face and laughed, crinkling her eyes. "What a way to wake up! You spoiled a perfectly wonderful dream."

As happy and peaceful as she looked, her words made me shiver. "What dream?" I asked.

"I was dreaming about the wolves. Your wolves I guess." She looked at me again, her face filled with wonder. "They were silvery and

71

beautiful. They were dancing around a clearing and calling me to come and play with them. That's where I was going in my dream. I was going to play with the wolves and learn their ways."

A bad chill settled over me as she described her dream. It wasn't the real wolves who sent dreams like that. It was the evil werewolves. They had tried to lure Kim out of her room and into the swamp where they waited for her with dripping fangs.

And they had almost succeeded.

But I couldn't explain all this to her. She wouldn't believe me. Or, even worse, if I told her about the werewolves, she would guess that I was one of them. How else would I know about their evil ways?

I couldn't let Kim find out I was a monster.

"Come, Kim," I said miserably. "We go inside now."

She nodded, already looking sleepy again. "Funny," she said. "I never sleepwalked before."

I shivered. Would I have to stay awake every night to make sure she didn't sleepwalk into the werewolves' trap?

We headed back to the house, Kim yawning and me worrying and feeling awful.

"Good night, Gruff," she said once we were inside the kitchen. "Thank you for waking me. I might have gotten lost in the woods if you hadn't." She smiled at me again and started upstairs.

"Good night, Kim," I said, turning back to lock the back door.

But as I clicked the lock I happened to look out the kitchen window. A black figure darted out of the shadows and slithered along the shrubbery toward the front of the house.

I gasped. The werewolf must have followed us! And I never even heard it or felt it.

Without thinking I yanked open the door again and ran out into the night.

Chapter 20

I ran to the front of the house, after the were-wolf.

But it had disappeared. I paused uncertainly, wondering which way to go.

A breeze sprang up and I tensed fearfully as the bushes alongside the house rustled as if something was moving around under them. Could the monster be hiding in the shrubbery, waiting to jump out at me as I passed?

Moving slowly, I peered into the bushes. I couldn't see anything but spreading patches of darkness. In order to make sure nothing was lurking there, I would have to crawl under the bushes.

I shuddered. I would be completely helpless crawling around blindly among all those branches. All the werewolf had to do was stay still and wait for me to come within its reach. Then it could grab me before I had a chance to cry out. And that would be the end of me.

And if the monster wasn't hiding in the bushes, if it had gone out to the street, it would get away while I was poking around in the shrubs. I decided to check the street first.

And there it was! A hunched figure was

lurching up the road, swinging its shaggy head. It was looking for prey, I was sure! If I didn't chase the creature, it might lure another child out of a house or reach through a window and snatch a sleeping baby.

My bare feet slapped the pavement as I ran after it. But the werewolf never looked back to see me.

As I gained on it, I started to feel nervous. What would I do when I caught up to it? I had no claws, no sharp fangs, no super strength. I couldn't attack it. I couldn't even stop it or scare it. Basically, I was monster food.

Slowing a little, I reconsidered. I needed a plan. Maybe I should just follow it. Then, when the werewolf tried to grab a child I could shout an alarm and wake everyone up. Yes, that's exactly what I'd do. Just keep the werewolf in sight and wait.

Great plan. There was only one thing wrong with it. The werewolf had just disappeared!

My heart began to pound. Speeding up, I ran as fast as I could to the spot where I had last seen the monster. But it was really gone.

My stomach shriveled with fear and worry. The werewolf could be inside any one of these houses. It could be creeping up on a sleeping child right now.

I had to sound the alarm immediately. I sucked in a huge lungful of air and opened my mouth to scream.

Out of the corner of my eye, I saw something big leap at me from the shadows. I screamed.

"AAE — "

The scream died in my throat as a large angry face suddenly loomed in front of my eyes.

"Mr. Clawson!" I gasped.

"It's the wolf-boy, isn't it?" demanded the school principal. "What are you doing out here this time of night?" His nostrils flared angrily as he stared at me, waiting for my answer.

"I-I-I saw something," I stammered. "In yard. So I follow."

"Humph," said Mr. Clawson. "Likely story. Wolves prowl at night, looking for prey, don't they? Is that what you were doing?"

He thrust his face into mine menacingly and I backed away. "No," I said. "No."

"It's a good thing I was out walking my dog," said Mr. Clawson. "Or who knows what new mischief you might have caused."

I shook my head, looking around nervously for his dog. The principal would be likely to have a dog that liked to bite boys, I thought. But I didn't see any sign of a dog.

"My dog ran off," said Mr. Clawson. "He

likes to chase things. Maybe the dog is what you saw — if you're not just making that up."

He frowned darkly at me and I backed up another step. "No," I said again. "I saw something."

Mr. Clawson nodded. "He's a big dog with a jaw full of teeth. You better watch out for him on your way home. Now, get along and don't let me catch you out here again."

"Yes, Mr. Clawson," I said, turning to go back the way I'd come. I was relieved to get away but a bad feeling nagged at me. It was something Mr. Clawson had said, something not quite right. But what? I just couldn't remember.

I hurried up the street, keeping a nervous eye out for Mr. Clawson's roving dog. But everything was quiet and nothing moved in the shadows.

When I got home I quickly let myself in and locked the kitchen door. I was so relieved to be there I just sagged against the door, letting the safe feeling of the house and the sleeping family settle around me.

But I still couldn't relax. Something was wrong. But what could it be?

The house was quiet and still. I chewed at my lip as I went slowly upstairs, trying to figure out what was bothering me. Then, just as I sank into bed, it hit me.

Mr. Clawson didn't have a dog! I sat bolt upright, staring into the dark. Miss Possum had told me he didn't have a dog. "Mr. Clawson doesn't like animals," she had said.

But if he wasn't out walking a dog then what *was* he doing?

Chapter 21

In school the next morning Miss Possum let me sit next to Paul in class.

I slipped into my seat feeling good. My reading lesson with Kim yesterday had me looking forward to cracking the books. I figured I ought to be able to sound out just about anything now that I had the alphabet sounds clear in my brain. Wouldn't Miss Possum be surprised!

But it didn't work out quite like that.

To begin with, she asked us to open our language arts books to page fifty-six. My heart sank right away. I didn't know how to count. I didn't even know what numbers looked like! I realized I had to learn a counting alphabet as well as a reading alphabet.

And then it turned out that hardly any words were spelled the way they should be. And everyone read along so fast they were done while I was still trying to puzzle out "thorough" in the first sentence. It seemed I really couldn't read any better at all.

So it was a tremendous relief when the bell rang and Paul told me to leave my books behind. "You won't need them for this next class," he said. "It's gym. No reading. No math. And no girls."

All the boys filed into a big room with a wooden floor and high ceiling.

"We're doing gymnastics," Paul told me. "Just watch the other kids and when it's your turn, do the same stuff."

"Sure," I said, but my spirits were plummeting. There was strange equipment all over the floor. I had never seen any of it before and it didn't help when Paul rattled off the names. "We've got parallel bars and a chinning bar and rings and a climbing rope . . ."

Right about then I forgot to listen. More boys were coming in and one of them sent my mood plunging the rest of the way down a bottomless pit. It was Rick, the kid who had tried to beat me up.

As soon as he saw me he nudged a pal and the two of them made a beeline right for me. "I thought I smelled something rank," sneered Big Rick. "I should have known it was the swamp-boy."

I turned away, pretending not to hear. I couldn't afford to get in any more trouble.

"Hey, I'm talking to you," said Rick, pushing me and knocking me into Paul.

Anger flared. I could feel my eyes blazing as I

started to turn toward Rick. But just then a man shouted, loud enough to drown out all the kids' noise.

"Okay, boys, line up. Two lines, hurry it up," said the man, walking briskly alongside the bustling crowd of boys.

"That's Mr. Grunter, our teacher," Paul whispered. "He's okay."

I forgot about Big Rick as I watched the first kids demonstrate their gymnastics. They scrambled up the climbing rope, hung from the rings, rolled over backward and forward, chinned themselves, and did awkward-looking tricks. It looked like fun. Now that I knew what the strange equipment was for, I couldn't wait to try it.

Then Big Rick started in again. "Hey, animal-boy," he hissed. "I hear you lap water out of the toilet bowl. How's it taste? Pretty good, huh?"

I pressed my lips together in a straight line and pretended not to hear. The boys in front of us turned around to see what was going on.

"Don't pay any attention to Rick," Paul whispered. "He's a fart-nose."

"What are you saying, Paul?" Rick taunted, coming closer. "I hear your mother puts newspapers on the floor so wolf-boy here won't mess up his water bowl."

81

I tried to shut my ears and concentrate on watching the class. But most of the class was watching me. And my fingers were balling into fists at my side. My breath was coming harder.

"Don't do it, Gruff," urged Paul. "Stay calm. Remember Mr. Clawson's detention. Nothing's worth doing that again, right?"

Big Rick swaggered closer, grinning around at his audience. "Human food makes animal-boy sick. But he'll eat anything, so he gobbles it up. And then he throws up on the floor. And then guess what he does?" Rick's grin got wider. "He licks up his own vomit!"

The other kids laughed. I kept my eyes facing forward. Anger buzzed in my head. My stomach felt hot and acidy.

"Actually, the worse thing is he's not even a wolf-boy. That wolf-boy stuff is just garbage. A pack of lies. Ain't that right, wolf-boy?" He sneered the last words into my face and I could smell his oniony breath. "You weren't raised by wolves, were you? I can see it in your face — you were raised by rats. Yeah, that's it, you're the rat-boy!"

I'd had it. Anger was a red curtain all around me. I didn't care about detention or what Mr. Clawson might do or anything.

I turned slowly toward Big Rick, my fingers flexing in spasms.

I'd teach him.

Rick looked surprised when I stared him in the eye. But he had a bigger surprise coming.

I raised my fists and charged straight at him.

Chapter 22

I saw Rick's mean blue eyes grow bigger with fright. He let out a startled squeak as I whizzed past, moving so fast my air-wake spun him around.

I leaped onto the climbing rope and raced up it, hand over hand, my feet not even touching the rope. Feet would only slow me down. At the top I pushed off, launching myself through the air and over to the rings.

The rings looked like the most fun. I slid down the ropes until I could pass my feet through the leather rings. I swung back and forth a few times, building momentum. Then I let go, throwing myself backward. My feet slipped out of the rings.

Below me I heard a frightened gasp. But the class seemed far away now. I was flying. It was like being in the trees with no extra branches to get in my way.

I flipped in midair and caught the rings with my hands.

Below me kids started to clap and stamp their feet.

My face flushed with pleasure. I swung a

couple more times and when I was good and high, I let go.

Paul cried out in dismay as I shot through the air, right over the floor apparatus. Another boy screamed. I felt like I was flying. Only the floor was coming up fast to meet me.

My stomach flip-flopped. Did I do this right? But there wasn't time to think.

I landed, just as I'd planned, right in front of the chinning bar. I let my motion carry me into a standing back flip and at the top of it, caught the bar with my hands. I swung around the bar a couple of times, keeping my legs straight and stiff.

Then I stopped at the top. My handstand was so steady my body hardly quivered. I balanced there, relishing the "oohs" and "wows" from the watching class.

How's that for an audience, Rick? I said to myself.

When I'd done the handstand long enough, I walked on my hands to the end of the bar, flipped around a couple of times and did the handstand thing again.

I let my weight carry me under the bar, let go at the top and rolled in the air, coming down perfectly astride the horse. I rolled off that and onto the parallel bars where I did some handstands and one-hand twists, then leaped up onto my feet and ran the length of each bar, like a tightrope.

I finished with a backward flip and came to a perfect landing in front of Mr. Grunter.

The teacher was trying to frown but there was an excited smile in his eye. The class stood in stunned silence for a few seconds and then burst out in wild clapping and cheering.

Mr. Grunter held up his hand for silence. "That was quite a display," he said. "Very skilled. Where did you learn all that?"

"In the woods," I said. "With wolf family."

"Very impressive," said Mr. Grunter. "But, you know, we have rules here. It wasn't your turn. Discipline is very important."

Paul came rushing up. "But Mr. Grunter, it was Rick's fault. He kept taunting Gruff, calling him rat-boy and trying to get him to fight. Gruff couldn't help himself."

I shot a fierce look at Big Rick. He dropped his eyes and looked at the floor.

"Is that true, Rick?" asked Mr. Grunter.

All the kids were staring at Rick now. He stuffed his hands in his shorts pockets and shrugged. "I was just kidding," he muttered.

Mr. Grunter nodded. "I see. Don't you think an apology is called for?"

Rick took a couple of steps forward, biting his lip. "I guess you're not a rat-boy," he said in a low voice.

"Is that all?" Mr. Grunter sounded steely.

"I'm sorry I called you names," said Rick grudgingly. "You really are a wolf-boy."

I wasn't sure how Rick meant that but Mr. Grunter nodded, satisfied, and Rick went back to his place.

"Class dismissed!" shouted Mr. Grunter.

I started to edge away but the teacher put out his hand. "Not you, Gruff. I want to speak to you a minute."

I waited as the class filed out. What did the gym teacher want with me? Was he going to give me detention after all?

Finally everybody was gone. Mr. Grunter started toward me across the gym floor. I couldn't tell a thing from his face except he looked very serious.

Then just before he reached me the gym door burst open with a bang!

Mr. Clawson strode in, his face purple with rage.

But there was a sly, secretive look in his eye.

Chapter 23

"I heard there was trouble in this class, Grunter," said Mr. Clawson, making straight for me. His heavy footsteps were loud on the polished floor. "I suppose this wolf-boy trouble-maker was responsible?"

He jutted his big jaw at me, looking pleased that I had messed up again.

"No trouble," said Mr. Grunter, moving to my side. "Oh, another boy was taunting him a bit, but Gruff proved he's got the right stuff." Mr. Grunter clapped me on the shoulder. "This boy knows how to channel his aggression into sports, Mr. Clawson. In my book he's headed for an *A*."

The principal frowned. Thunderclouds of displeasure formed over his eyes. He jerked his head at Mr. Grunter. The gym teacher gave me a reassuring look, then followed Mr. Clawson to the side of the room.

Mr. Clawson spoke rapidly for a few minutes but, of course, I couldn't hear a word. All I could do was watch Mr. Grunter's face anxiously. He looked concerned, then alarmed.

When Mr. Clawson finished talking he shot one fierce look at me across the room, turned on his heel and left. Mr. Grunter came slowly toward me, scratching his head in puzzlement.

"The principal is worried about you, Gruff," said Mr. Grunter. He didn't seem nearly as pleased and enthusiastic about me as he had a few minutes ago. "He says you have a wild imagination and violent tendencies."

He paused, as if what he had to say next was even worse.

"Mr. Clawson thinks you'll have to be locked up during the full moon. Now why would he think that, Gruff?"

Chapter 24

That night I sat at my bedroom window, keeping watch. But no men slipped down to the woods to change into werewolves. No monsters prowled the yard and taunted me. No dreams came to lure Kim from her safe bed.

At school I kept quiet, trying not to be noticed. The other kids looked at me funny sometimes but at least Miss Possum didn't say anything more about making me leave sixth grade. Every day after school, I practiced talking and reading and writing. I even learned some arithmetic.

And every night I kept watch at the window. It was exhausting.

But after a couple of weeks when nothing happened, I started to think maybe the werewolves had gone away. They knew I was onto them so maybe they decided Fox Hollow was too dangerous for them. Maybe they'd moved to a town where no one suspected there were monsters roaming the night.

But meanwhile the time of the full moon was coming closer. And when the full moon rose I would become a monster, too. Before that happened I would leave this house and my new family and disappear into the swamp. Deep in the swamp I would hide until the beast in me was driven out. I would never harm the people of Fox Hollow. I would never let them learn my true nature.

That's what I promised myself.

Then one night I fell asleep in my chair at the window.

And when the moon rose, my eyes popped open. The moon hung as yellow as a plump lemon in the sky. The light was cool on my face but every muscle in my body was coiled tight as a spring.

I jumped up from my chair and leaned forward to look out the window. What had awakened me? Was it a werewolf?

The backyard was quiet. No one was on the street. But the hairs on my arm prickled as a distant sound reached my ear.

"Aaaaaaooooh. . . . . Aaaaaaooooh. . . ."

The howl of the werewolves!

Then I saw something dash across the backyard. A werewolf? It ran into the road and I saw it was only a dog. But the sight of the dog jangled my nerves.

There was something I had to do. I'd put it off as long as I could. I had to find out if Mr. Clawson really had a dog.

I jammed on my sneakers — I was dressed except for them — and quietly slipped out of my room. Before leaving I checked Kim's room. She was sleeping peacefully.

Nobody woke as I tiptoed downstairs and let myself out. Locking the back door behind me I pocketed the key and set off. Out on the street I paused to gaze up at the house.

It was my home now. I felt safe there, even loved. Inside, life was peaceful.

But the Parker family was in great danger. I looked up at the golden moon and trembled at the thought of anything harming them.

They didn't know a monster lived in their midst. Me.

But I wasn't the worst of the nightmare. Oh, no. It would get worse.

Much worse.

Chapter 25

Keeping to the patchy shadows, I made my way to Mr. Clawson's house. The moon was bright and I didn't want anyone seeing me.

But as I sneaked along, scurrying from the shelter of a tree to the shadow of a bush, I wondered if what I was doing was foolish as well as dangerous.

Maybe there was nothing sinister about our school principal. It could be just like Mr. Clawson had said — that he thought I was a trouble-maker and he didn't want trouble at his school. He hadn't said two words to me since that day at the gym when he told Mr. Grunter I might need to be locked up during the full moon.

And since then I'd been careful to do nothing that would attract attention. I'd stayed away from Rick and studied hard.

If Mr. Clawson was really concerned about protecting his students, maybe he'd had an instinct about me. Even normal humans could sense dangerous creatures. Mr. Clawson might have sensed the beast in me right from the start.

Sure, the werewolves prowled Fox Hollow in the darkness. But maybe I was the only monster who lived right in the midst of the unsuspecting people.

I turned down Mr. Clawson's street, feeling sneaky and low. All the houses here were quiet and dark, just as they were all over town. Mr. Clawson's house was the same as the others, no different.

And then I heard it. So close I almost jumped out of my skin and into the tree I was hiding under.

A howling!

"Aaaaaaooooooooooooooo . . ."

Chapter 26

I peeled myself away from the tree as the mournful howl died away in a series of rough barks.

I sighed with relief. It was only a dog. A big powerful dog, from the sound of it, but still only a dog.

So Mr. Clawson had a dog after all, I thought. Miss Possum was wrong about him — Mr. Clawson did like animals. And I must be wrong about him, too.

I wanted to see the dog with my own eyes but I hesitated. It sounded mean and dangerous. What if it attacked me? What if Mr. Clawson found me here, messing with his dog?

I knew I should go home but I just couldn't. Now that I was here I was determined to scope out that dog. There was an oak tree at the edge of Mr. Clawson's yard and the animal's howl came from that direction. Hunching low, I scurried along the front of the house to the shadow of the oak tree. If the dog ran at me I could always climb the tree to safety. Probably even Mr. Clawson wouldn't think to look up into the branches of a tree.

I peered into the moonlit shadows behind Mr. Clawson's house. A black shape moved. A chain rattled. I breathed a sigh of relief. The dog was chained. Boldly. I moved a little closer, out from under the safety of the tree.

Then I stopped, cold bumps raising on my arms and legs. The dog was chained in the yard of the house next door. It wasn't Mr. Clawson's dog after all!

Before I could dart away, back to the deep shadows under the oak tree, the big dog whined in fear. I froze. A large twisted shape crept out of the dark, toward the cowering dog. It snarled, softly and viciously.

The dog yelped and threw itself into the air, away from the menacing figure. The chain clanged as it stretched to its full length and yanked the dog backward. The dog fell heavily to the ground, yelping and whining madly.

The menacing shape threw back its head and laughed gleefully.

My blood ran icy in my veins. I felt paralyzed. I knew that sound. Then the creature turned its head and I saw the glow of its fiery red eyes. It was a werewolf!

I didn't even dare breathe. Cold shivers ran down my back all the way to my toes. I felt moonlight pricking at the hair on my head. All the creature had to do was look my way and it would see me for sure.

The dog heaved itself up and ran again until again the chain jerked it back, almost choking it. The poor animal was crazed with fear.

Luckily for me the werewolf was so involved in teasing the dog it didn't seem to know I was there. I forced myself to move, inching back into the shadows as the monster flicked its tongue and swiped its claws at the frenzied dog.

Slowly I moved, trying to make myself invisible as I crept back under the oak tree. When I felt its trunk against my back I grabbed hold of it and swung myself up into its lower branches.

Just in time. In the street another pair of red eyes glowed like wildfire. The second werewolf swiftly crossed the lawn toward the first. And then I saw another, its eyes burning holes in the night.

And then came another. And another.

They met in the moonlight, hissing and spitting at each other.

There were werewolves everywhere.

Then one of them lifted its snout and sniffed the air suspiciously. Its scraggly fur bristled. Baring its long yellow teeth in a snarl it began to turn toward the oak tree I was hiding in.

The werewolf had scented me!

Chapter 27

I clung to the trunk of the tree with all my might. My insides were quivering.

Sniffing, the werewolf took a step in my direction.

I looked up into the tree, wondering if I could escape by climbing higher. The branches were thick and close together and the leaves would hide me. The creature might scent me but it wouldn't be able to see where I was.

Carefully inching my way up the trunk I reached for the next branch. But as I started to pull myself up there was a sudden outbreak of noise on the ground. My heart lurched sideways in my chest. Were they all after me now?

Flattening myself against the tree trunk, I peered through the leaves. The werewolves were prancing and jumping excitedly. The creature that had been sniffing around my tree had gone back to join the others. All of them were staring at something on the ground, their red eyes glowing so hot they seemed to spark in the cool air.

I gasped as a human head slowly appeared,

coming up out of the ground. A man's shoulders followed. The werewolves fell silent, except for an occasional hiss of excitement — or was it fear? The air around me crackled with electricity.

As the man rose out of the earth, he raised his head. Moonlight fell on his face, and I saw it was Mr. Clawson! I clenched my teeth to keep from crying out.

Then Mr. Clawson stepped up onto the lawn and I saw it was only his cellar he'd come out of, not the ground itself. So there was still a chance he was only human. I realized my fingers were numb and loosened my grip on the tree. My muscles ached from tension but I didn't dare move.

The werewolves gathered around him, circling and murmuring. Mr. Clawson snapped his fingers at them and they spat and cringed away. Ignoring the werewolves, Mr. Clawson lifted his hands toward the moon.

His whole body shuddered. He seemed to swell with strength.

The monsters snarled and hissed as if they'd like to tear him to pieces — if they weren't so scared of him.

But they *were* scared. Even the evil werewolves shrank in fear from him. Then Mr. Clawson threw back his head and a great roar issued from his thickening throat.

I stared in horror as I recognized what he had become!

Chapter 28

The grass burned where Mr. Clawson's long yellow fangs dripped saliva onto the ground. He dropped to all fours as muscles rippled along his back and legs. Thick gray hairs sprouted all over his body as his clothing burst at the seams and fell away.

Mr. Clawson, our school principal, was the biggest, most dangerous of the monsters who had chased me through the swamp. He was Ripper, the leader of the werewolves, the one who had found me the night of my first wereing. It was Ripper who tried to make me kill. Once I tasted blood I would be like them — like him — forever. I had escaped him once but could I do it again?

Watching him change, I trembled with fright. He was so strong and I was so small and weak. How could I ever stop him?

Once the Change was complete Ripper sucked in a huge lungful of air and rose up on his hind legs. The other werewolves gathered around him, cringing from the reach of his long curved claws. They waited for his command.

Ripper's burning eyes stared them down. When all the werewolves were still as death,

101

Ripper opened his great jaw, showing rows of glistening razor-sharp teeth.

His words echoed inside my head.

"My brothers, the time is soon. On the first night of the full moon we will take the children of Fox Hollow. Our bite will free them. Their blood will be our blood. There can be no escape."

As these terrible words burned into my brain, a silent cheer went up from the listening werewolves and pounded in my head.

"We must be ready," thundered Ripper, although the sleeping people of Fox Hollow would hear no sound. *"Each of you knows what to do."*

"YESSSS!" screamed the werewolves inside my head. They began dancing with glee around their leader but stopped the instant he raised one claw-tipped hand.

"Go!" Ripper commanded. He took a step forward. The werewolves scattered out of his path, leaped into the air, and disappeared into the night.

The great werewolf Ripper stood motionless, the moon spilling cold light over his shaggy head and muscled shoulders.

I held my breath. What was he doing?

Ripper raised his head and shot one burning

glance into my tree. I pressed myself against the rough bark, faint with terror. He knew I was here! He took a step toward the tree.

His voice boomed in my head. *"There will be no escape!"*

He lifted his hand and slashed at the tree. Tiny bits of shredded leaves rained down onto the ground.

In another moment he would rip me out of the tree.

Chapter 29

Then Ripper suddenly turned on his heel and strode away from me and the tree. His evil laughter trailed out behind him, fouling the air.

He disappeared down into Mr. Clawson's cellar and the night was still again.

My knees were knocking so hard I couldn't immediately climb down from the tree. I don't remember how I got home or up to my bed. But I know I didn't sleep.

Tomorrow is the first night of the full moon, I kept thinking, numbly. Tomorrow. When the moon rose, I, too, would become a monster but I could no longer run off to the swamp and leave my new friends in Fox Hollow. There was too much danger.

"We will take the children of Fox Hollow," Ripper had promised. But he hadn't said how. And I was the only one who could try to stop it from happening.

The next morning, first thing when I got to school, I went to Miss Possum. She took one look at the dark swollen circles under my eyes and bent her head with concern.

"What is it, Gruff?" she asked. "Is something wrong?"

"Terrible things," I said in a rush, encouraged by the sympathy in her kind face. "Werewolves. Coming. Tonight. You must believe. Must help." I struggled with the effort to find the right words. Even though I could understand almost everything and could even read some now, it was still hard for me to sort my thoughts into words. "They come at full moon. Children in danger. Please. We must stop them."

Miss Possum's soft brown eyes widened. She looked very alarmed. I felt a surge of hope. "Dear me, Gruff," she said. "I know it's been rough for you being thrust into civilization so suddenly. And I've been very impressed with your progress. Very impressed. But it's only natural the strain should take its toll. You're anxious about fitting in, Gruff, and it's made you imagine these terrible things."

Miss Possum patted my head reassuringly. "You must try not to worry so much. You'll get used to us humans," she said. "And, Gruff? One thing I can tell you for a fact. There's no such thing as monsters."

It was no use, she'd never believe me.

I chewed my nails until gym class and then I tried Mr. Grunter. I had become one of his favorite students since it turned out I was good at almost all gym things. This time I tried a slightly different tack.

"Remember last full moon, Mr. Grunter? Wolves blamed for bad trouble?"

He nodded, looking at me curiously. "Sure, Gruff. Be pretty hard to forget that."

"Not wolves. Werewolves," I said, shaking my head for emphasis. "Werewolves coming tonight. Coming for children."

Mr. Grunter scratched his head thoughtfully. But just then Mr. Clawson appeared at the door of the gym. "You ready, Grunter?" asked the principal. "We're about set to go."

Mr. Grunter waved, calling back, "Sure thing." Then he turned to me. "What you say is interesting, Gruff. I must admit, I always wondered why a wolf would come through a window after a child. But we don't have time to discuss it now. Come see me after the field trip, and we'll discuss your concerns."

"Field trip?" My voice squeaked. The hairs on my neck began to rise.

"Sure, isn't it great? The principal organized a surprise field trip for the whole class. Quite a treat." Mr. Grunter grinned and hoisted a backpack onto his shoulder. "We're leaving as soon as the bell rings."

"But no!" I cried. "Mr. Clawson is werewolf. Mr. Clawson is leader!"

But my words were drowned out by the loud clanging of the bell.

Chapter 30

Kids were pouring onto a waiting school bus as I ran outside. Kim and Paul waved at me as they climbed aboard. "Come on, Gruff," they called, faces flushed with excitement.

"No! Don't go!" I screamed, running alongside the bus. "It's a trap! They'll get you! Monsters will get you!"

Kids looked at each other in surprise and then began to laugh. "Good one," someone yelled. "Monster stuff!"

"No," I yelled. "Really! It's true. Werewolves coming. Horrible danger!"

But the kids laughed louder. "Werewolves!" I heard them hooting. "It's broad daylight, we're getting to go on a field trip instead of spending the day in school, and Gruff is talking about werewolves! What a funny kid."

My heart thudded in my chest. I felt so helpless.

A heavy hand came down on my shoulder. My heart leaped into my throat. I whipped around, knowing who I would see.

"I guess this means you don't want to come with us on this field trip," said Mr. Clawson, his eyes blazing into mine, his fingers digging into my shoulder like he was itching to rip me apart right there. "Well, that's fine," he snapped. "You can stay right here. In the basement, perhaps." He paused to consider it. "Yes, I think so. Your own special detention room in the basement."

I jerked away from him, my breath coming in little gasps. I turned and ran. As fast as I could go, I ran after the bus.

"Wait! Wait for me!" I couldn't let them face the monsters alone.

The bus puffed black smoke as it pulled away from the curb. It was leaving without me. "Wait," I screamed. "Wait."

But the bus kept going.

Chapter 31

I raced after the bus, waving my arms and shouting. I saw kids waving back at me and laughing. Slowly, with a grinding of gears, the bus ground to a halt. Mr. Grunter, who was driving, opened the door.

"Decided to come with us, did you?" he said, grinning at me. "You won't regret it, Gruff."

I dropped into the seat behind Kim and Paul. They twisted around, still laughing.

"We thought you weren't coming," said Kim.

"I know you want to stay in school and learn all the stuff you've missed, Gruff," said Paul, his blue eyes twinkling. "But werewolves — that's going too far even for you."

My stomach lurched as Big Rick dropped into the seat beside me. He was grinning. "Hey, geek-face, that monster stuff was pretty cool," he said, jabbing an elbow in my ribs. "Did you see Clawson's face? He looked like he had a mouthful of old roadkill."

"He *is* roadkill," chimed in another kid.

"Come on, you guys, he's the one who organized this field trip," Kim protested. "Give him a break. Mr. Clawson got us out of school for the whole afternoon. He can't be all bad."

"Oh, yeah? The monster stuff may be weirdsville but wolf-boy's right about one thing," said Rick. "Clawson never did anything because it was going to be fun for us kids. He's got something up his sleeve. For instance, why won't he tell us where we're going?"

"He wants it to be a surprise," said Kim.

"That's what worries me," said Rick. He stood up and pointed out the front of the bus, at a large black car with heavily tinted windows that was leading the way. "Clawson won't even ride on the bus with us. He can't stand kids. His idea of a surprise is not going to be our idea of fun."

"He's probably taking us to the state prison to show us what happens to bad kids who don't follow all his rules," chimed in Paul, looking worried.

"What spoilsports you guys are," said Kim, tossing her head and making her hair swing over her shoulders. "I'm not going to listen to this anymore." And with that she started singing at the top of her lungs:

"A hundred bottles of puke on the wall, a hundred bottles of puke. One of the bottles of puke fell off, ninety-nine bottles of puke on the wall, ninety-nine bottles of puke . . ."

It was a funny song and educational, too, with all the counting. I wanted to join in but I felt like something furry with teeth was gnawing on the inside of my stomach.

It was two o'clock in the afternoon. In five hours the full moon would rise. The wereing would begin.

Mr. Clawson would become Ripper, leader of the werewolves. He would have the children of Fox Hollow right where he wanted them — trapped far from the safety of Fox Hollow and their parents.

We drove for a long time. Big Rick amused himself by singing loudly in my ear and leaning heavily against me every time we went around a curve. I gritted my teeth and ignored him. I had bigger things to worry about.

Finally the kids on the bus got tired of the puke song and began to guess at our destination. "The state park!" "The wax museum!" "The beach!"

Suddenly the bus lurched. Kids were thrown against the sides. The bus jolted and wobbled. Something scraped the roof.

I jumped up to see what was happening. The principal's black car had turned onto a narrow dirt road enclosed on both sides by thick trees and brambles. The road looked like it hadn't been used in a long time.

The bus was turning into the woods, following the black car.

"Don't!" I shouted. "Don't follow. We'll never leave! Don't follow, he'll get us!"

Chapter 32

Mr. Grunter looked at me in his rearview mirror and laughed. "Of course we'll follow Mr. Clawson," he said. "He's the principal. We have to do what he wants. Now sit down and be quiet, Gruff. Everything's going to be fine. Don't worry."

Don't worry!? The trees closed in around us, so thick and dense they turned day into night. Branches scraped the windows and snapped under the wheels of the bus. Leaves hid the rest of the woods from view. This wasn't a place I had ever been before.

"Well we're not going to the beach," muttered Rick, slumped in his seat. "Or the state park or the wax museum."

"Or the prison," snapped Kim, turning around to scowl at Rick. But her eyes widened as she looked at me. "Gruff! What's the matter? You look so gloomy."

I could only shake my head. I felt so totally helpless and lost. We were heading into a nightmare and nobody would believe me.

"It's only a field trip, Gruff," said Kim reassuringly. "We'll go for a walk in the woods and identify some trees and some birds maybe.

114

You'll be right at home here. You'll know twice as much as the rest of us," she said, trying to cheer me up.

She looked so friendly and honest and worried for me. But I had a terrible secret I couldn't share. If Kim knew about me, the monster inside me, she'd run screaming in terror.

Already, with the shadows closing in and the smell of the swamp growing stronger, I could feel the power of the moon pulling at me. Would I be strong enough to resist?

I remembered the power of the wereing. When the beast had hold of me, would I be strong enough not to harm my new friends?

"What's with you, wolf-boy?" Rick challenged me, jumping as a tree branch knocked against his window. "All this gloom and doom stuff is giving me a pain. You afraid of the rabbits, maybe? Afraid of the squirrels? Or are you just squirrelly?"

I didn't answer. The smell of the swamp was filling the bus now. It was the boggy smell of mold and things that lived a long time ago in places where the sun never penetrated.

No, it wasn't birds and rabbits that scared me. It was red eyes that glowed in the night. And two of those eyes were mine.

115

Branches whipped by the windows of the bus and I just watched, paralyzed. I couldn't come up with a plan to defeat the werewolves and there was no way I could convince any of these jumping, yelling, happy kids of the danger they were heading into.

But finally the joking and laughter died down. Maybe it was the jolting of the bus, which creaked and groaned every time it hit a rut or rolled over a stone. Or maybe it was the darkness of woods so thick they shut out the sun. Or maybe it was the strange and ancient swamp smell, so alien from the air of the town. Whatever it was, everybody seemed pretty subdued.

Even Rick stopped bumping against me every time we bounced over a rut in the dirt track.

Finally the bus slowed and slowed and shuddered to a stop. Sunlight! All the kids leaped up from their seats to see where we were. But there wasn't much to see.

We were in a small clearing, surrounded on every side by trees and thick brush. Kids looked at each other and shrugged and sat down again. "Why are we here?" someone asked. But no one had an answer.

The bus door opened. Mr. Clawson climbed inside, looking pleased with himself.

"All right, students," he said. "This field trip is about learning to appreciate your environment. Mr. Grunter and myself will point out many species of plants and animals along the trail. The trail itself winds through woods and swamp. Some places are boggy and dangerous, so stick to the trail and follow me at all times."

He glared. "Got that?"

Everyone swallowed nervously and nodded. "Yes, Mr. Clawson."

"There's a wonderful variety of wild creatures living right here just a few miles from Fox Hollow," Mr. Clawson went on with a secret smile. "And once the daylight fades, the swamp really comes alive!"

The principal's eyes gleamed. His stare fell on me. A red glow flashed. "You'll be amazed at what comes out of the swamp at night. Just amazed, isn't that right, Gruff?"

His eyes blazed on me as he grinned, showing me a glimpse of his sharp teeth. I jumped up from my seat. I couldn't help myself.

"Don't get off bus!" I cried, looking wildly at all the kids around me. I grabbed Paul's arm. "Don't go! If you want to live, stay here!"

Chapter 34

Mr. Grunter's strong hands grabbed hold of me. He held me up in front of Mr. Clawson as easily as he'd grasp a sack of potatoes.

Mr. Clawson clucked his tongue and shook his head sympathetically. "Poor boy," he said. "Clearly unbalanced. Perhaps it was too soon to bring him back to the woods. But we can't let one boy ruin the whole field trip, can we?"

How could it be that no one else saw the twitching claw at the end of the finger he pointed at me?

"This is really too bad," said Mr. Grunter with a sigh, shaking his head at me. "What should I do with him?" he asked.

"Lock him in my car," said the principal, his eyes flashing red again. "He'll be safe there. Safe enough."

Mr. Grunter nodded and led me off the bus. I looked back. Kim and Paul were glum and sad. But I could see they were just worried that I was crazy. They still didn't believe a word I'd said about the werewolves!

Still holding my shoulder carefully, as if he thought I might bolt or turn around and hit him or something, Mr. Grunter brought me to the black car. He opened the back door and nudged me inside.

"Sorry about this, Gruff," said the gym teacher. "But it's not often Mr. Clawson takes the kids out of school. They'd all be pretty upset if we had to cancel the field trip on account of you. But you'll be fine here. Maybe you can take a nap until we get back. It won't be more than a few hours. 'Bye, Gruff."

Mr. Grunter locked the car carefully and pocketed the keys. All the kids had already filed off the bus and formed two lines at the head of the trail.

With Mr. Clawson leading, they began to head down the trail and into the swamp.

My chest tightened. I began to feel like I couldn't breathe. I banged on the window with my fists and yelled for them to stop. But the car was so heavily built, no one could hear me.

A few kids looked back before they disappeared into the woods. Kim and Paul waved in my direction, looking sad. I pressed my face against the car window, begging them not to go.

But I knew they couldn't hear me. The windows of the car were so darkly tinted, they couldn't even see me.

A moment later all the kids were gone, as if the swamp had swallowed them up.

I stared after them in disbelief. The monsters were going to get them and I was locked up in a metal box. Frantically I began pulling at the door handle next to me but it wouldn't budge.

I had to get out of here.

The clearing was deathly quiet. And the sun was going down.

Chapter 35

There were no lock buttons on the tops of the doors. It was as if the car had been specially made to hold prisoners like me.

I had to break a window. Lying down on the backseat, I drew my legs in. I shielded my head with my hands to protect it from shattering glass. Then I kicked out, slamming my feet into the window as hard as I could.

Pain shot up my legs from the impact. But my feet bounced off the window harmlessly. I stared in disbelief. What kind of window could be that strong?

I kicked again, even harder. And again and again until my legs were numb with pain and I was out of breath. The window wasn't even cracked. I tried the rear window and the windshield but they were made of the same tough material.

Panic rose into my throat. I couldn't be trapped here. I couldn't! I leaned forward and buried my head in my hands. But no great ideas came to me. In frustration I began to pound my fist on the flat area between the two front seats.

SNICK!

I was making so much noise I almost missed it.

SNICK, SNICK, SNICK!

Little buttons had popped up on each of the doors. The lock buttons! I must have accidentally banged the control that worked all of them. Mr. Clawson probably figured the wolf-boy was too dumb to find the switch. And he was almost right.

I slid over and tried the door handle. The door swung open. Fresh air poured over me. I leaped out of the car as if I thought it might lock itself up on me again.

There was no time to lose. The sun was below the tops of the trees. The light was fading fast.

I took off down the trail, following the kids, straining my ears for some sound of them.

But the swamp was quiet. Too quiet. Where were the birds and squirrels?

A creepy feeling slithered down my spine. Something didn't feel right. But I knew I was on the trail of my friends. I could see their footprints. I could smell their human smell.

Smell them? I stopped, the hair prickling on the back of my neck.

And suddenly a snarling beast exploded out of the underbrush! A blur of fur and claws, it leaped straight for my face!

Chapter 36

I ducked, throwing up my hands and letting out a shout. The creature screamed and shot over my head.

I whirled and saw its ringed tail disappearing fast into the bushes. It was only a raccoon. But it had been terrified of me. Of me!

I looked up, dreading what I would see. The sunlight was completely faded now and the shadowed twilight was deepening into night. I saw a faint yellow glow over the tops of the trees on the far horizon.

My breath caught in my throat. That glow was where the moon was rising. I was running out of time. When the moon's rays touched me I would change into a werewolf.

Already I could feel my senses sharpening. I heard a mole digging furiously to escape deeper into its burrow. High in an oak, a baby bird cheeped in distress.

Blood pulsed harder in my veins. I had to get to my friends before I became a monster. They'd never believe me then.

There was no more time to lose.

I took off up the trail, feet pounding as hard as they would go. I knew if I didn't get there in time Mr. Clawson would change into Ripper and — but I couldn't think about that.

Suddenly I heard someone cry out up ahead. It was a whimper of pure fear. Somehow I put on more speed, ran even faster. My heart banged in my chest. The cry came again.

And then a voice. "Don't be scared of the dark, little one." It was Mr. Clawson's voice. "The night is your friend," he said soothingly. "And I'm here. I'm *heeere*." Mr. Clawson's last word stretched into a growl. It sounded as if he could hardly keep himself from changing into Ripper right that second.

But I was almost there. I'd save them. They were just around the next bend. I could hear them all now.

"Where are we?" I heard Kim ask, her voice sounding shaky. "We're not lost, are we, Mr. Clawson?"

The principal laughed. It sounded throaty and thick, not quite human. "Lost? Of course not."

I rounded the bend and there they were! I opened my mouth to shout and slipped on a patch of dead leaves. I went down on one knee.

As I scrambled up, a shaft of moonlight broke through the trees and struck me right between the eyes.

Chapter 37

Bright light blinded me. My head seemed to glow from within. I shook my head to clear it and moonlight poured into me like an electrical charge.

I fell to the ground as if I'd been struck by lightning. Power surged through me. My skin rippled as new muscles ran under the surface like rope. My fingers clenched and claws sprouted, long and beautifully curved.

Fangs erupted from my gums. My teeth grew long and pointed. My nose lengthened into a snout and a world of marvelous smells opened up to me.

RIIIIP!

My clothes fell away as muscles tightened and swelled my strong body. My skin toughened into fine hide and fur sprouted to cover it. I tasted the night with my tongue. My eyes sharpened and glowed until I could see an ant scurry off the path and a moth flutter through the trees.

I was strong, magnificent and free. No one could touch me.

But then I heard one of the kids whimper again. "I want to go home," she wailed.

And I remembered who I really was and why I was there. I had to warn everyone what was about to happen. I had to get them out of the woods. Confidence flowed through me. I was strong, I could save them.

Opening my jaws to shout a warning, I was suddenly struck dumb. As a werewolf I had all kinds of powers. But one thing I couldn't do was speak in the human tongue. I couldn't shout a warning or tell my friends how to save themselves.

Mr. Clawson had won after all. I stamped my foot into the ground and raged in misery and frustration. I gnashed my teeth and howled in fury.

"AAAAOOOOOOOOOOOOOOOOOO!"

Instantly fifty heads snapped in my direction. I felt the silvery glow of the moonlight shimmering on my powerful new body. Someone screamed. And then everyone was screaming in fear. The piercing noises hurt my ears.

I clapped my hands over my ears and slunk out of sight into the woods.

"What was that?" shouted Big Rick.

No one answered him.

And then I had an idea. I knew how I could save the kids. I'd scare them right out of these woods.

Chapter 38

I slipped through the woods, my feet flying over the ground. I felt my body glowing in the moonlight. My skin tingled deliciously as if silver light ran in my veins instead of ordinary blood.

But I was so hungry. Hunger gnawed at my stomach. A pheasant, too terrified to stay hidden, burst from the bushes, flapping wildly. I could snatch it from the air with one swipe of my claws. My fangs dripped as I pictured how sweet the bird would taste.

But no. I remembered what Ripper had told me during the last full moon, when I became a monster for the first time. *"After your first kill, little one, you will be one of us."* I shuddered. No matter how hungry I was, I didn't dare kill anything, not even a mouse or a pheasant.

I would never be one of the werewolves. Never.

I swallowed my hunger and raced on, circling around behind my school friends. If I was going to scare them, I wanted them running back toward the bus, not deeper into the swamp where the werewolves were waiting.

Reaching the trail, I headed toward them,

baring my fangs in the moonlight. I could hear the kids' voices, frightened and confused.

"Hey, where's Mr. Clawson?" cried Paul. "He was here a minute ago."

My heart skipped and thudded in my chest. If Mr. Clawson had slipped away then it might already be too late. The werewolves would attack at any second!

I leaped into a bright patch of moonlight and howled, beating my breast with hairy fists.

Chapter 39

Kids scattered, screaming, in every direction.

Oh, no! This was not what I wanted. If the kids didn't stick to the trail they would get lost in the woods, fall into bogs of quicksand, be caught by werewolves.

"Stop!" shouted Paul. "Everybody! This way. Back to the bus!"

"Right," yelled Kim, grabbing the arm of a boy who was running the wrong way. "This way!"

The boy set off back to the bus and most of the kids turned and followed him. A girl, screaming in terror, stumbled off the path, and Kim pulled her back, shoving her in the right direction. "Come on, everybody," she cried. "Stay on the trail. Stick together!"

She and Paul went after the kids who had fled into the swamp and herded them back to the trail.

"I think that's everybody," said Kim, panting with exhaustion and covered with mud.

"I think so, too," said Paul, scratched and equally dirty. "Let's get out of here."

I crouched in the underbrush, letting them get a little ways ahead of me before I followed, so the sight of me wouldn't frighten them half to death. But I needed to follow, to make sure the werewolves didn't ambush them along the way. I was just starting after the group when I heard the cry.

"Help! Heeelp!"

It was a boy's voice. One of the kids was still in the woods and he sounded weak. I looked after my friends, racing as fast as they could back to the bus. If I left them now, the werewolves might attack. But I couldn't abandon anyone who was crying for help.

Gnashing my fangs in worry and frustration, I bounded into the woods, toward the sound of the cries, away from my friends.

"Heeeelllp." The hoarse cry was fainter.

I leapfrogged a small tree and sailed over a stand of pricker bushes, landing beside a thick mud bog. Even with my werewolf sight, I didn't see the boy right away. He was almost over his head in the sucking mud. Then I saw a pale white hand grabbing at the air. His upturned face gasped for breath. He was at the far side of the bog, only a few feet from dry land.

I cleared the bog in a single jump and landed softly beside the struggling boy just as the mud closed over his head. Grabbing hold of a sapling on the bank I stretched myself out over the pool of mud. I reached for the boy's hand but his mud-slick fingers slipped from my grasp.

I held my breath and stretched further, but the boy had sunk beyond my reach. A bubble of mud burst on the surface. I stared in horror. I had to get him out.

I slid down the bank a little further. The sapling whipped out of my hand and I fell face forward in the mud. But I didn't sink. Quickly I thrust my hand beneath the surface of the oozing mud. I felt the boy's wrist and grabbed it, holding on tight.

Careful not to shred his skin with my claws, I hauled his head above the surface so he could breath. The boy coughed and sputtered, shooting mud in every direction. As the moon fell on his face, I was startled to see it was Big Rick!

As he breathed in huge rasping gasps, he began to struggle again. I felt the sucking mud creep up my sides. This worthless bully was going to get us both killed! Anger and fear spun like a whirlpool in my stomach. I hissed warningly at Rick.

He went instantly rigid. As he tried to turn his head to see who was saving him, I let go of his wrist and yanked him by the hair. He tried to scream and a gob of mud stuck in his throat. As he choked I wriggled backward through the mud, dragging us both inch by inch.

But his heaving body was pulling me down. Mud lapped at my snout and crept over my back. I tasted the stinking mud on my tongue. Fear prickled along my spine.

But my werewolf leg muscles were strong. I gritted my sharp teeth, dug my toe claws into the bank and pulled. With a mighty effort I heaved Rick up out of the mud and tossed him toward the bank. Gripping the dry earth with my toe claws, I worked my way out, hauling Rick up onto the bank.

He lay, eyes tight shut, chest heaving, unable to move. But I was aware of every precious second that passed. While I was stuck here with this bully, my friends were in deadly danger.

Where were the werewolves? Of all the animals in the swamp, they were the only ones that could hide from my sharp senses. I couldn't catch the secret scent of a werewolf and when they wanted to disappear into the shadows I couldn't see them until their horrible eyes flashed red.

I growled in frustration. I couldn't leave Rick here — I'd have to carry him.

At that moment, Big Rick stirred and

groaned. He opened his eyes. Seeing me inches from his face, he came instantly to life, sparked by pure terror. He let out a shriek that hurt my ears and scrambled to his feet.

Mud flew in every direction as he ran. Luckily he was heading back toward the trail so I didn't have to do anything but growl once or twice to keep him running fast.

Back on the trail I could hear the kids arguing. They were still heading toward the bus but their progress had slowed dangerously.

"We'd already be back at the bus by now if this was the right direction," said one girl.

"I say we find Mr. Clawson and Mr. Grunter," a boy suggested.

"Let's face it," said a tall kid. "We spooked ourselves in the dark woods and got panicked into seeing things. Now we're lost. I say we stay right here and keep shouting for Mr. Clawson to come get us."

"We're not lost," Paul pleaded. "It's just a little further."

Just then Big Rick burst on the scene, coated with mud and spouting gibberish. "A monster — fangs — kill us!" He kept running, his hair standing in stiff spikes, and set off a ripple of panic among the kids.

"Stay together!" yelled Kim.

"Run!" shouted Paul. "Let's get to the bus!"

I loped along after them, close behind but keeping out of sight along the edge of the trail. They could make it to the bus. Once the door was shut, they should be safe. Now if only they would keep running so I wouldn't have to howl and scare them all again — I hated that.

I had my eyes trained on the kids and forgot to watch the woods around me. That was a mistake.

I was just thinking they were all going to make it out safely when a shadow moved.

Suddenly a huge fanged shape leaped out of the woods.

I tried to twist away but the thing was too quick, too big.

"OOOOMPH!"

The full weight of the beast smashed into me and knocked me across the trail.

Then it had me pinned flat to the ground.

Chapter 40

The werewolf's foul breath stung my eyes and burned the inside of my nose. My throat closed up as I struggled to heave it off me.

But strong claws pinned me to the ground. It hissed and I heard its voice inside my head. *"You can't move, little Gruff. There is no escape."*

Ripper!

I stopped struggling and the werewolf leaned back a few inches so the moonlight fell on its hideous face. Red eyes glowed with fury. Its lips parted in a snarl. I couldn't help myself cringing at the sight of its needle-sharp fangs.

Ripper growled ferociously. The torn remnants of Mr. Clawson's suit clung to his arms and legs in shreds. He leaned into my face again and his claws dug deeper into my shoulders. It stung like fire where his claws pricked and I felt my blood bubble and hiss from the wounds.

"The children belong to us!" Ripper's voice scraped the inside of my head. *"Join us! Taste blood tonight or die!"*

"NO!" I screamed with all my force, bucking my back up off the ground. I twisted and

heaved the monster off my chest. His claws raked my shoulder and at the fiery pain I brought my hands up and threw him off me.

That took Ripper by surprise. I could see in his maddened eyes that he wasn't used to anyone fighting back. Before he could stagger up I leaped into a tree.

Ripper swung around, snarling. His spit flew, burning everything it touched, like acid. *"I'll get you,"* he thundered inside my head.

Terror made me super fast. I swung from one tree to the next, racing through the leafy branches after my friends. I could hear them shouting and crying in panic as they stumbled along the trail. They were almost at the clearing.

I felt the werewolves gathering below, looking for me. They sniffed the air and lunged at shadows.

All around me I could feel the heat of their glowing red eyes. They gnashed their teeth and struck out at one another in frustration. Howls of pain and fury filled the night.

But there was something else, something worse. It was like an evil shimmer in the air or a bad, sickly smell that came from all directions at once. It needled at the back of my mind like a thorn I couldn't reach.

What was it? Was I forgetting something?

And then suddenly I knew what it was I was sensing. It hit me like a kick in the stomach.

It was the werewolves' hunger. More than anything they wanted to feed.

Chapter 41

I reached the clearing giddy with panic. But Kim and Paul were there, herding the other kids onto the bus as fast as they could.

"Hurry," said Paul. "Move it. We'll be safe on the bus."

Kim comforted a girl who was crying. "We made it," said Kim. "We're back at the bus and we're all here. There's nothing to be scared of now. Nothing can get us inside the bus," she repeated, helping the girl up the stairs.

In a rear window I could see Big Rick's white face pressed up against the glass, huge eyes swiveling back and forth through the trees, looking for monsters.

"But who's going to drive us out of here?" wailed a boy, shivering violently while he waited his turn to board the bus. "We lost Mr. Grunter and Mr. Clawson!"

Kim and Paul looked at each other and looked away quickly. They didn't want to think about what had happened to their teacher and their principal. "Let's just get on the bus first," said Paul gruffly. "We'll think about what to do once we're all safe inside."

"They'll be along soon," Kim said in a quavery voice. "Mr. Clawson and Mr. Grunter are probably right behind us, trying to figure out what kind of animal was chasing us. They'll be here in five minutes and probably make us feel silly for running away."

Kim looked like she was trying really hard to believe this. I made sure I stayed out of sight in the trees, my eyes roving the dark edges of the clearing for signs of werewolves.

My ears pricked up at a stealthy movement in the woods behind me. Careful to make no sound, I turned on my branch and peered down through the leaves. Nothing. I moved along the branch, searching the ground where the noise had come from. But all I could see were tree trunks and bushes.

Then I heard a disgusting drooling and slurping. My flesh crawled. My eyes darted to the spot and found a shadow that was not the shape of the tree beside it. I tensed, every muscle ready. Out of the dark, red eyes flashed for just an instant.

But it was long enough. Opening my powerful jaws, I growled viciously and sprang from the tree. The startled werewolf hissed in fear and leaped into the air, spinning away from me.

"GRRReeeeeeeeee!"

My claws raked its leg and it howled in pain

as it fled deeper into the swamp, away from the clearing and the children.

Anger pumped through my body as I looked around for more of the werewolves lurking in the shadows. I began to circle the clearing, keeping hidden in the trees, a low growl rumbling in my chest. But I saw no more flashes of hot red eyes in the dark.

Then, as I finished circling, I heard a clumsy noise deeper in the woods. I stopped, fur bristling. Something grunted and stumbled. It was coming this way.

I threw a glance over my shoulder. All the kids were now on the bus. Paul was struggling to get the door closed. I was torn. It seemed important to find out what was crashing around in the woods but I didn't want to let my friends out of my sight. What if it was a trick?

CRASH!

"Ugggh!"

Every muscle ready for battle, I sniffed the air. The scent of the thing was familiar. I sniffed again, puzzled. A human! Mr. Grunter!

Instantly I set off running through the trees. Our gym teacher must be hurt. I had to help him!

Soon the clearing vanished in the dark behind me. My heart soared. Mr. Grunter could drive the bus! He could save the kids from the werewolves.

I raced, the cool night breeze stirring my fur. Ahead of me came another groan and I slowed. I didn't want to scare Mr. Grunter to death at the sight of me. But how should I approach him? I couldn't talk, to tell him not to be frightened.

I reached up, pushed aside a branch and there he was. Mr. Grunter was staggering as if there was something wrong with his leg. And he seemed confused, as if he didn't know where he was.

I started creeping slowly toward him, a plan forming in my head. I could grab him from behind and cover his eyes with my hand so he wouldn't see me. Then I'd carry him to the clearing and let him go. From there he could make it onto the bus and he'd never know the horrible sort of creature that saved him.

But just as I was reaching out for him, Mr. Grunter turned and the moonlight fell on his face.

I gasped in horror. Half his face was human but stretching and swelling, bones pushing out under the skin! The other half was covered with patchy grayish fur. One eye was blazing red.

As his red eye fell on me, Mr. Grunter's lips pulled back over his teeth. Long yellow fangs glistened in the silvery light.

Mr. Grunter was turning into a werewolf!

Chapter 42

"Gruff, wait!" cried Mr. Grunter, the words mushy in his half-human mouth. One leg ended in a human foot, the other was sprouting horny claws.

RIIIIP!

Mr. Grunter's human clothes popped at the seams and fell to the ground as the change became complete. Now both eyes blazed red and I heard his words only inside my head.

"We won't hurt the children," he insisted, reaching toward me with his clawed hand. *"We're only going to help the children become like us, Gruff. Then the town will be ours! We'll be free! You can't stop us so you might as well help."*

I stepped back from him. The kids! Mr. Grunter had lured me away from the bus! I spun in the air and set off running back to the clearing.

Mr. Grunter sprang after me.

"You know how good it feels to be one of us, Gruff," his werewolf voice cried inside my head. *"Humans are weak and puny. They can't smell the creatures in the woods. They can't hear the pulse of life in the wind. Let the chil-*

dren be bitten so they can feel our strength. Let them be like us," Grunter pleaded, flaring his werewolf nostrils. *"Think how wonderful it will be when we can all run together. All hunt together!"*

"All kill together," I snarled, kicking him away from me. Finally the clearing was in sight. I could hear kids moaning in fear. Some were crying.

All around me I began to hear the hissing and snapping of werewolves gathering.

"Please Gruff," whispered Grunter. *"You can't stop them. Don't go against Ripper. Save yourself!"*

He reached for me and I spun away, sprinting across the clearing. Werewolves were beginning to howl with excitement.

I bolted for the bus. Catching sight of me, the kids inside began to scream. I leaped on top of the bus and crouched, ready for battle.

Hot red eyes advanced through the night toward the bus. They looked like bobbing coals, staining the night red. As the creatures emerged from the swamp into the clearing, moonlight fell on them.

I sucked in my breath, frozen at the awful sight of so many of them. It was an army of monsters. Their yellow fangs dripped with anticipation as they advanced. Their glowing eyes were focused completely on the children in the bus.

Leaping over their heads from out of the darkness, Ripper landed in front of his followers. He threw back his huge head and howled.

"AAAAAAAAAAAAOOOOOOOOOOOOO!"

It was the signal for the attack to begin!

Chapter 43

The werewolves charged. For an instant I was paralyzed by the sight. Their hot eyes blazed. Razor-sharp claws and long dripping fangs flashed in the moonlight. The earth shook under the thunder of their running feet.

Shrieking and howling filled my ears as the monsters swarmed over the bus, their claws clicking and scraping along the windows. One of them leaped to the roof of the bus and grinned at me, fangs dripping.

With a tremendous roar I threw myself at it and hurled it off the bus to the ground. Growling with triumph I watched it bounce, a look of horrible surprise on its ugly face.

But I watched too long. A claw ripped into my shoulder from behind. As I howled in pain the werewolf leaped on my back. It aimed its claws at my face, trying to blind me. I bent over, like I'd learned in gym class, and flipped the thing off my back, sending it hurling off the roof.

I spun around at a sound on the metal roof. Another werewolf, grinning. I knocked it off the roof before it could spring at me but when I turned, another was already in midair, aiming for my head. I somersaulted and kicked up with my legs, giving it a push that sailed the monster right over the other side of the bus.

Under my feet I could feel the kids panicking and hear them screaming.

"We've got to get out of here!" yelled Big Rick, starting a stampede for the door. "They're going to get us!"

"No!" shouted Paul at the front of the bus, blocking the door. "Remember what Gruff said. He said to stay on the bus and now we know we should have listened to him, right? So let's stay together. We'll be safe here. If we go running into the night these creatures will just pick us off one by one." He turned to Kim as Rick backed away. "At least Gruff is safe locked in Mr. Clawson's car. Nothing could get to him there."

Grunting, I tossed another werewolf over the side and then had to fight off two, coming at me from opposite directions. I got them to charge and then ducked so their extended claws sank into each others faces. But more creatures were coming at me.

How long could I keep this up? My muscles hummed and sizzled with the excitement of the fight but I could feel myself getting tired. I bared my teeth as I jumped into the air to hit a charging monster in the stomach with both feet. I'd just have to keep going — all night if that's what it took.

But suddenly I heard the sound of shattering glass. A triumphant howl went up from the crowd of werewolves.

They had smashed the windshield of the bus!

I ran across the roof to the front of the bus. Already werewolves were swarming over the hood toward the broken window. Their snaky tongues hung over glistening fangs and their red eyes blazed with glee, like neon blood.

The bus wasn't enough to keep the children safe. And I was only one, while they were many.

I'd fight to the end but I knew the end was near.

I threw back my head and let out a long, mournful, lonesome howl of defeat.

"AOOOOOOOOOOOOOOOOOOOOOOOOO!"

Chapter 44

"AAAAAAAOOOOOOOOOOOOOOOOAA-
AAAOOOOOOOO!"

My ears pricked up at a howl in the distance. An answering howl. It was a beautiful, round, night-filling sound, nothing like the howls of werewolves.

Could it be? I stood high on my hind legs, nose quivering.

"AAAOOOOOOOOOOOOOOO!"

Yes! The wonderful howling came again, closer this time, and I knew. It was a wolf, a real wolf. And not just any wolf — it was Wolfmother!

The werewolves on the hood of the bus slid off to the ground. The creatures banging at the windows of the bus let their hands fall to their sides. The monsters stood waiting, glowing eyes turned to the swamp.

Again, Wolfmother howled that she was coming.

Could the werewolves understand as I could? One or two looked around uncertainly. The rest stood without moving as if riveted in place, staring into the dark.

Inside the bus, the kids stopped screaming. Their wondering faces appeared in the windows.

Everyone was waiting. Waiting to see what would happen.

Chapter 45

The night grew very still. The werewolves stirred uneasily. A sound, like wind rushing through the trees, came toward the clearing.

Blood dripped down my shoulder and I scarcely noticed. Bruises and wounds stung and ached but all I was aware of was the thrill of excitement that ran up and down my spine. Wolfmother was coming!

And suddenly she was there. Silently, without warning, the wolves burst into the clearing. Real wolves! Magnificent wolves!

It was a huge pack, with Wolfmother in the lead. I had never seen so many wolves before. Every one of them was big, beautiful and silver in the moonlight.

The werewolves shrieked and huddled together as the wolves overflowed the clearing. Still silent, the wolves ringed the clearing, eyeing the hideous monsters. Then Wolfmother tossed her head and the wolves attacked without warning.

Werewolves shrieked and scattered. Jaws snapping, the wolves tore into the monsters, ducking under their claws. Fur flew. Howls filled the air. For a few seconds werewolves and real wolves were just a blur of motion.

Anxiously I searched the tangle of ferocious animals for Wolfmother. Was she all right? Was she hurt?

But I couldn't find her. The wolves were strong and there were a lot of them but they didn't have supernatural powers. I was afraid the werewolves would destroy them. I had to try to help Wolfmother.

But I couldn't see a good spot to jump in.

Suddenly the tangle of bodies broke apart. I saw Wolfmother! She was snapping at the heels of a fleeing werewolf.

I stared, amazed. All of the werewolves were fleeing! Running and leaping as fast as they could go, the werewolves were escaping into the swamp in all directions. They were shrieking in terror!

The werewolves were afraid of the wolves!

But as I stared, feeling joy swell in my chest, a voice ripped into my head. *"Traitor!"* it screamed.

Ripper! His fury shook my mind like a handful of marbles. I moaned and fell to my knees.

"We'll get you for this!" hissed Ripper, venom dripping from every word. *"I'll get you!"*

154

Chapter 46

The shrieks of the werewolves faded away into the swamp. Ripper's voice vanished from my head but the pain and shock made me feel fuzzy. I got clumsily to my feet, shaking my head to clear it.

Down below, the wolves were running around the edge of the clearing, tails high, nostrils flaring.

Inside the bus, the kids broke into a riot of cheers.

"Yea, wolves!" they yelled, clapping their hands. "Way to go!"

"Get those ugly monsters, wolves! Sic 'em!"

They whistled and laughed and hooted for joy but the wolves paid no attention whatsoever.

My legs suddenly felt wobbly with relief. I moved across the roof to jump down and go to Wolfmother. But then I hesitated. Real wolves did not like werewolves. Wolfmother had brought the pack to help the children but that did not mean she wanted to see me — not when I was a monster like the others.

I searched the crowd of wolves, looking for

her. But as I showed my face several of the wolves began to growl, their neck fur rising threateningly.

Then one of the wolves shot out of the pack. With a tremendous spring, he leaped into the air and landed beside me on top of the bus.

The wolf growled ferociously, showing his teeth and I began to shiver. It was Sharpfang. My brother. His eyes looked into mine and they were as cold as February ice.

I wanted to tell him who I was but of course I couldn't. As a monster I couldn't make wolf-speak any more than I could humanspeak. Then I had a horrible thought. Maybe Sharpfang already knew who I was. Maybe it didn't matter to him anymore.

Sharpfang growled again and tensed himself to spring at my throat. I couldn't move a muscle.

Chapter 47

I closed my eyes and scrunched them tight.

Waiting seemed to take forever. Then something big landed softly beside me and I heard the click of wolf claws on the metal of the bus roof.

Startled, I opened my eyes. Wolfmother stood beside me, bristling at Sharpfang. She barked sharply and my wolfbrother dropped out of his attack stance. But he wasn't happy about it. He glared at me and backed up without taking his eyes off mine.

Wolfmother came close and made a small sound in her throat. She looked into my eyes and I saw sadness there. She knew who I really was!

I was so happy to see her and I'd missed her so much. Without thinking I reached out to touch her. Sharpfang growled a warning but Wolfmother ignored him and took another step toward me. She shivered as my claws brushed her fur but didn't move away.

I settled my hand on her back. My heart bubbled over with love. But I could feel her trembling under my monstrous paw. She knew I wouldn't hurt her but it was against all her instincts to let a monster like me touch her.

Something seemed to break in my chest and flood my insides with warm liquid. I felt the muscles of my hideous face tighten and stretch. What was happening to me?

Liquid fogged my keen eyes and splashed down my hairy cheeks. I was crying! Great monster tears rolled down my face. Wolf-mother raised her head and licked the tears from my cheeks.

I'd never be a wolf and maybe I'd never be a real boy. But I was human enough to cry.

Sharpfang barked softly. The moon was setting and there was a hint of dawn light in the sky.

I watched the wolves until the last tail disappeared silently into the swamp. Then I slipped off the roof of the bus and, slinking under the windows so none of the kids would see me, I went back to Mr. Clawson's car where, somehow, despite everything that had happened, I fell deeply asleep.

Chapter 48

I couldn't have slept long. When I woke the sun was just beginning to rise over the trees. Birds sang in the woods once again and my terrible hunger was gone.

I was a boy again. A boy with no clothes!

I jumped up. My clothes were in the woods where they'd fallen from me when I changed into a werewolf. Well, I couldn't go back and get them, that was for sure.

Luckily Mr. Clawson kept an extra set of clothes in his trunk — probably for emergencies just like this one. His pants were miles too big but I tied his shirt around me like a loin cloth, just like I used to do with animal skins when I was a wolf-boy.

The bus was still closed up tight, except for the smashed windshield. I walked over to it and knocked on the door.

It opened instantly. "Gruff!" Paul pulled me in and slapped me five. "We thought you were okay locked in Mr. Clawson's car, but there was no way to check. You sure were right about those monsters. How did you know?"

I shrugged, then Kim ran up and hugged me and I didn't have to answer. "It's so good to see you," said Kim. "We were so scared. But you're all scratched and bloody! And what happened to your clothes?"

My heart sank. I didn't want to lie. But I couldn't tell the truth.

"Wow, those horrible things must have got you after all," said Paul, going pale. "Was that when you howled for the wolves? When those *things* pulled you out of the car and ripped off your clothes?"

I nodded, unable to speak. But I noticed Big Rick giving me the fish eye. He was suspicious.

"We must go," I said, trying to change the subject. My throat felt raw and my tongue seemed even more awkward than usual. "Come. It's a long way. We must be out of woods by dark. Not safe after dark."

"How do we know it's safe now?" demanded Big Rick, frowning. "How do we know you won't lead us right to those — things — whatever they are?"

"Gruff tried to warn us," Kim said, going right up to Rick. "We were the ones who wouldn't listen. He knew about the werewolves from living in the swamp with the wolves, right Gruff?"

I nodded. "Yes," I said, grateful I didn't have

to try and explain it myself. "Come. We must leave here."

"But what if they get us while we're in the woods?" cried a girl I didn't know.

"Daylight safe," I told her. "Night is dangerous."

"Our parents are never going to believe any of this," muttered another kid.

"They're going to be really worried by now," said someone else. "We better get going like Gruff says."

"But what about Mr. Clawson and Mr. Grunter?" said another. "They never came back."

"They both werewolves," I said.

The kids stared. But none of them seemed all that surprised. After that they followed me out of the bus although I could tell some of them were still afraid to leave.

"The wolves were so beautiful," said Kim in a wondering voice as we started down the path toward the road. "That was your old family, wasn't it?"

"Yes," I said, my voice thick.

"They rescued us because you called them, didn't they?"

I nodded.

Kim bit her lip and looked at me sympathetically. "And they left you behind," she said. "You must be sad."

"A little," I said, fighting back tears. "But glad, too, to be with you and Paul."

And that was true. My heart ached thinking I might never see my wolf family again but I was so happy that I'd helped save my human friends. Even though I was a monster.

But I was one other thing, in addition to being happy and sad.

I was scared. Because that night the moon would rise. And I knew absolutely without any doubt that terror would come again.

Ripper's words rang in my head like an echo of doom. *We'll get you,* he'd promised. *I'll get you!*

And I knew he'd be back, as soon as the moon rose.

Don't Miss
THE WEREWOLF CHRONICLES
Book III: *The Wereing*

Ripper rose up, towering over the werewolves.

"You all know our mission. You know your places and your roles. We will not fail! During the next full moon we will turn every human in Fox Hollow into a werewolf — all those we don't want to eat, that is!"

A chorus of cackles erupted but cut off abruptly when Ripper raised his paw. "One kill you leave to me. And we all know who that is."

"GRUFF!" shouted the werewolves, making my blood turn to ice and my knees to jelly.

But Ripper wasn't finished. *"Remember, all the people of Fox Hollow must be made werewolves. Then WE control the town. After that, we'll march on — to the next town! And the next! And the next! Now, get to work!"*

The other werewolves began howling a

chant, leaping onto their chairs, cackling and snarling. *"We want the world and we want it NOW!"* they shrieked.

They hurled themselves onto the table and huddled together. Then all at once they raised their hideous snouts into the air and began to howl at the top of their lungs.

"AAAAAAAAAAAAAAAAAAAAOOOO OOOOOOOOOOOOOOO!"

About the Authors

RODMAN PHILBRICK and LYNN HARNETT are the authors of another popular Apple Paperback series, The House on Cherry Street. Rodman Philbrick has written numerous mysteries and suspense stories for adults, and the much acclaimed young adult novels *Freak the Mighty* and *The Fire Pony*. Lynn Harnett is an award-winning journalist and a founding editor of *Kidwriters Monthly*. The husband-and-wife writing team divide their time between Kittery, Maine, and the Florida Keys.

The evil is coming.
In fact, he is already here!

THE WEREWOLF CHRONICLES

The Wereing

The Werewolf Chronicles Book III

By Rodman Philbrick and Lynn Harnett

Coming to a bookstore near you.

We have to be careful. So careful that we can't trust anyone.

ANIMORPHS

I started the morph. My skin turned gray. My legs became a powerful tail. Believe me — I didn't really want to go out to the middle of the sea. But lately I've been having weird dreams about the ocean. Something is calling me. And that's why I'm morphing into a dolphin. Finally, my hands become fins . . . and I'm gliding through the water.

ANIMORPHS #4: THE MESSAGE

by K.A. Applegate

Step Inside a Morph. It'll Change Your World.

THEY'RE COMING SOON TO A BOOKSTORE NEAR YOU

AN1296

Phantom Rider Rides Again!

GHOST VISION

Phantom Rider
by Janni Lee Simmer

*C*allie knows she's the only person who can see Star. But lately the ghost horse has been appearing at odd times and in strange places—like in front of Callie's school. And Star is starting to look sick. Can Callie find a way to help Star before she fades away forever?

Appearing soon at a bookstore near you.